ALL THE SMALL WONDERFUL THINGS

ALL THE SMALL WONDERFUL THINGS

Kate Foster

CANDLEWICK PRESS

Copyright © 2021 by Kate Foster

First US edition 2023
Originally published as *Paws* by Walker Books Australia 2021

Library of Congress Catalog Card Number 2022922777
ISBN 978-1-5362-2580-8

23 24 25 26 27 28 APS 10 9 8 7 6 5 4 3 2 1

Printed in Humen, Dongguan, China

This book was typeset in Plantin Infant MT Std.

Candlewick Press
99 Dover Street
Somerville, Massachusetts 02144

www.candlewick.com

For Harry

MONDAY, NOVEMBER 7

Five days to PAWS

CHAPTER ONE

Jared's giving me the look. I'm pretty good at recognizing the signs now.

A light breeze tickles my cheeks, and I lift my chin, letting it cool my sweaty neck. Distracted, I wonder if it might be cooler inside the classrooms than outside today—probably even cooler than here in the shaded area, actually. It's a hot day for November, though I can't remember the weather on all the days in all the Novembers I've been alive.

I glance away from Jared's freckly face and his flushed, pink cheeks and concentrate harder on my mouth and my voice, on finding the right words to tell him about how far I got on *Tunnels of Disaster and Doom* Map Five and the forty million new Orbsicles I won last night, but I can't stop my eyes from moving back up to him.

He's looking over my shoulder at the kids playing on the field, and his feet and hands are shifting and fidgeting. This all tells me he doesn't want to be standing with me anymore and that his ears aren't listening to what I'm saying.

It's the same look most people get when I'm telling them about *OrbsWorld.*

But I absolutely have to finish telling Jared about *Tunnels of Disaster and Doom* Map Five. *OrbsWorld* is my favorite computer game ever, and last night I was messaging Jared—username rugballlove4578—and he's already completed Map Five, *and* he's the most popular boy *and* the best sprinter in the whole school!

I decide to talk faster.

". . . and it was that ladder that I got stuck on every time for, like, two weeks, but then I figured it out and—"

"Mm-hmm."

I recognize these types of response because of Mystery Game number three, and I know to watch for visual clues like body language and facial expressions because of Mystery Game number four. I learned all of this at the Be Aware classes I went to last year with Mum, Dad, and Ned. There were other families there with autistic children like me who also needed help understanding things like body language and emotions. Mum said we were lucky to live close enough that we could attend. I liked the classes, but right now, I'm not so sure they were helpful. Because the problem is, I don't know how to make Jared interested in what I'm saying, so I just keep talking.

"I had to climb the ladder halfway . . ."

"Yep." Jared takes three small steps backward, wiping his hands on his shorts.

". . . and then hop onto the platform when the ants—"

"Oh yeah." He adjusts his watch.

"Um . . ." My brain has stopped working and the right words aren't coming. "When, when the ants charge down the wall and, um, then I—"

"Okay, good job for doing it, Alex. I gotta go." Jared runs off, legs and arms pumping and his last words carried back to me on the humid air.

He charges across the shaded area and onto the grass, weaving through a group of girls singing and a game of handball between Isaac and Frank on the concrete and the new kid with white hair sitting alone on the swing. Now Jared's calling for Henry to pass him the ball. Henry's dodging Rahul, his hands waving in the air, his brown hair flapping beneath his blue cap. The sun beats down on all of them, but not on me, not where I stand in the shade.

The shouts and pounding feet of the other kids are suddenly loud.

5

Too loud.

I didn't hear them when I was telling Jared about *Orbs World*, about *Tunnels of Disaster and Doom* Map Five, but now the noises make my breathing go funny, and I wince.

Two kids, Joshua and Wu, rush by, Joshua roaring something to Wu that goes through my left ear and comes out my right, and I startle, my tummy lurching, a squeak escaping my mouth.

My eyes burn and I want to cry. But I won't, not here. Not now that I'm in grade six. So I press the feeling back down into my tummy and put my hands over my ears.

I want to shout at them, all of them, particularly Joshua and Wu, but Ned tells me I can't stop people from running and shouting and doing other things like that at lunchtime or recess. Ned says that policing people is bad and will get me picked on at secondary school—even though Ned is forever telling *me* what to do. But Dad always agrees with him and then tells me how rough his school was when he was a kid, and Mum gives me a sad smile, which makes me angry because I know it means she agrees but also feels sorry for me, because Mum feels sorry for me about everything.

None of them think I listen or see or understand,

but I do—mostly. That's a little bit because of my autism, which I know now because Mum explained how it doesn't always look as if I'm listening or following the way other children do. But I listen better when I'm drawing or on my laptop.

So I don't shout at Joshua and Wu. Or go after Jared and try talking to him again. Because even though I might not always say the right thing or think the right thing or do the right thing, I don't want to be beaten up or shouted at.

I'm not stupid.

I spin, the gravel crunching under my feet, and my left heel slips out of my black leather shoe because the laces came undone earlier. I need to tuck the ends in before I trip, because I can't do laces properly, but I don't. Instead, I head toward my classroom, hands still over my ears, because all the noises and the rushing children are pushing up a scream, and a sob is rising into my chest.

Ms. Westing and Mum say I can always head to the classroom if I can't regulate my emotions, and right now I can't. My coping beaker, the name we use for all the feelings inside me, is full full full.

Pale blue uniforms blur in my vision, and screeching voices and vibrating footsteps shudder through me, so I focus on my laces, the black strings

7

like two skinny snakes attached to my shoe, flicking back and forth. I don't like snakes, but I'm more scared of spiders. Though the dangerous ones like the redbacks stay hidden away, the orb weavers and the huntsman spiders are big and fast and make huge webs in trees and bushes everywhere, and they give me the creeps.

I hate spiders but I love dogs. Especially *my* dog. And Kevin, my cockapoo, and I have been working on a plan, something that will definitely make Jared, and maybe the other popular kids, want to be my friend. If I can't be good enough at *OrbsWorld* or fast enough at running, I only have one other chance, and that's Kevin.

I want to go home now and see him, but I can't. Mum doesn't come and get me anymore. She probably would, but Ms. Westing doesn't call her every time school becomes too loud for me or something happens that makes me emotional. They decided this without me—even though I was there in the meeting—at the beginning of this term, my last-ever term at primary school. They decided I had to try harder to handle the difficult times because secondary school would be even tougher.

I'm nearly at my classroom, the sounds of the other kids fading behind me. I take deep breaths, just like I've been taught—in through my nose and out through my mouth. My reflection floats along beside me in the windows of the grade six classrooms, all of them decorated in colorful artwork—sea creatures made with bottle tops, handwritten school rules on cardboard cut into flower shapes, night city scenes in black and red paper.

I like art and I love sketching Kevin and Dennis, Ned's lazy bulldog. I have a green robot notebook almost filled up with my newest dog sketches.

Thinking about drawing dogs makes me calmer. Plus, it's quieter at this end of the school. My classroom is at the end of D block, beside the new tree garden.

I should've stayed in the tree garden today, like usual, but Jared accepted my friend request on *OrbsWorld* last night and we traded Orbsicles for rations, so I thought . . .

I sigh and remove my hands from my ears, then sit on the chipped green bench outside my classroom. An ibis wanders past, pecking at schoolbags in search of leftover snacks. Lucky dinosaur bird. He can leave school whenever he wants. I hate school so much, but I hate the thought of secondary school even more, because I'm afraid of the big kids and all the noise and the extra homework and the strict teachers.

But most of all I'm afraid of never having a real-life friend.

CHAPTER TWO

Mum pulls into a nearby parking space in our Mitsubishi Outlander—my favorite car. Dad's silver truck is dusty and loud and bumpy, and I don't like it. She's late, which is normal, because she has to collect Ned from secondary school first, even though it would be quicker for him to walk here because his school is just on the other side of the lake. There's always traffic, she says, so I should never worry that she won't come—she'll always come.

Before I approach the car, I double-check the color and the license plate to be completely sure it's Mum. It is.

I push off from the black barred fence and adjust my bag on my back, then swig from my aqua water bottle as I walk over. Ned pokes his tongue out at me from the front seat. He's so rude to me. Mum says that's because he's fourteen and fourteen-year-olds don't always think. She says that he actually loves me and is trying to have fun.

"Don't *do* that," I say, and slap a hand on the

window. Mum jabs a finger at the back seat, her lips pursed, so I open the car door and throw my bag across the seat.

Coldness and quiet envelop me as I poke my head inside.

"Hey, Alex," Ned says, swiveling in the front seat and taking out one of his earbuds.

"Don't hit the car windows, please," Mum says, peering over her sunglasses at me.

"Why didn't you bring the dogs?" I ask, clambering into the car.

"Because." Mum shakes her head and turns toward the front again.

Is she cross with me? I don't think I said anything rude.

"How was your day?" Ned asks.

I reach out to shut the car door and a bike whizzes by.

"Bye, Al," a voice calls.

It's Tony, cycling home. "Bye, Tony."

Tony's nice to me but he's not in my class anymore, so he isn't my friend. He was last year, when I was in 5T, but now I'm in 6W with different kids. I didn't know all of them when the year started, but I do now. Most of them are nice to me, and I'm happy I don't have Ryan in my class, though he's always around at recess and lunch. Ryan says I can play with him on some days but not others and whacks my cap off my head and takes my pencils. That's why I don't do drawing at school anymore and keep my sketches a secret. Ryan doesn't do this every day, but he does it some days. Mum says it sounds like he has some problems too, but I don't behave like that, so I'm not sure.

I yank the door closed, shutting out the voices and the noises of car and bus engines, then secure my seat belt until it clicks, pushing it down to make sure it's definitely, definitely locked in.

"Alex, Ned asked how your day was." Mum flicks the turn signal, *tick tick tick*, and then joins the traffic leaving school.

"Yeah," I answer, breathing in the berry scent from the car air freshener.

"So rude," Ned mumbles, and turns back to the front.

What? "I'm not rude. I said yeah." My day was good, I think. I can't remember much of it, apart from Jared not wanting to be my friend again, so I don't know what else to say.

"You are," Ned replies, staring down at his

phone—probably at a *Fight Forest* live stream, Ned's favorite game. "I asked you how your day was and you just said yeah."

I screw up my face, ramming my lips together as Mum says something to Ned, her voice low. I can hear my mum and brother talking, but not the actual words, so I watch out the window as kids in Jessops Lake Primary School uniforms walk home with their parents and teachers in orange vests wander up and down the path by the crossing . . . and then I see it. The huge white poster tied to the school fence at the corner.

I see black and red lettering. The hand-drawn picture that changes every year, because it's chosen in a competition—this year the winner was a Chinese crested dog drawing—and then photos of a German shepherd, a poodle, a golden retriever, and a pug. An illustrated bunch of balloons. And the best words ever, which I've read every day since the poster first appeared thirty-two days ago.

"Go slow, Mum!" I yell, pressing my nose up against the glass. She tuts, and I read it as quickly as I can as our car rolls slowly past, anxious not to miss anything. I need to read all the words—all of them—and I'm not the fastest reader. I don't like reading at all, but I like reading these words.

PAWS
AUSTRALIA'S BEST DOG SHOW

(AS SEEN ON TV!)

JESSOP LAKE SHOWGROUND

SATURDAY, NOVEMBER 12

10 AM TO 4 PM

REGISTRATION GATES OPEN AT 8 AM!

DOG PARADES! COMPETITIONS! STALLS!

POLICE DOGS! PERFORMING POOCHES!

SEE YOU THERE!

I notice how they've missed the *s* at the end of Jessops and tap my teeth in irritation, but then I read the smaller black letters at the very bottom, the bit that makes the insides of my tummy twirl.

REGISTER YOUR DOG IN ONE OF
OUR CONTESTS BEFORE 10 AM!
EVERY WINNER RECEIVES A TROPHY AND GIFT.

PAWS is coming to Jessops Lake, which is where I live! A real-life, actual dog show. And this is the best dog show ever. It's the same one I watch on TV every year, the one that travels around Australia. I've wished super hard for six years and two months, since I was five years and five months old, that PAWS would come to a town on the Gold Coast, and this year, the year I turned eleven, the year I graduate from Jessops Lake Primary School, my wish has come true.

CHAPTER THREE

I thump the bed beside me and then hold my breath and squeeze the tightest fists I can until my fingernails bite into my palms. It hurts, but I keep doing it, squeezing harder and harder. I growl at my computer screen.

"Why? Why did you push me off? Now I have to start all over again!"

I can't believe dododeadbird5 just knocked me off the spinning ladder. Now I have to start over, and I was so close to the platform I always reach on *Tunnels of Disaster and Doom* Map Five.

"AGH! AGH!" I squeeze my fists even harder.

If I can get past the platform with the ants, I'll get another forty million Orbsicles, and then I'll get to figure out what to do next. If I make it to the end, I'll move on to Map Six and get to attend the fair. I'll be able to play with rugballlove4578 there and maybe trade more of my Orbsicles with him. Then maybe he'll let me sit with him at school.

Tears pool in my eyes and my neck hurts. I unclench my fists and rub the side of my neck with one hand, grabbing my mouse with the other.

"Alex!" Mum calls from outside my bedroom door.

"What?"

My door opens and Kevin trots in, bringing with him the sound of Ned's rap music escaping from his bedroom across the hall and the smell of lasagna—I know it's lasagna because each night's dinner is always written on the chalkboard in the kitchen. Kevin leaps onto my bed silently and begins licking my face.

Kevin is a cocker spaniel mixed with toy poodle. He's small, barely as tall as my knee, and not heavy. His tongue and his nose are cold, and his licks are fast across my eyelids and nose and cheeks. Dad says dogs like the salty taste of sweat and tears. Mum says they sense when you're sad or angry and want to make you feel better by licking.

I think they're both right.

I put my hand on Kevin's snout and push him back. His white fur is wet under his mouth, which means he's probably just had a drink, and soft on top of his nose. I'm surprised he's not sleeping after all the training and running practice we did in the yard earlier.

"Stop screaming like that. It's just a game, for goodness' sake." Mum stands in the doorway and

I glance up at her. One of her hands rests on the silver doorknob and the other grips a reindeer tea towel. There are dark splotches on her pink T-shirt.

"Why are you using the Christmas tea towel? Christmas isn't for another forty-eight days. What's on your top?" I add, frowning. Kevin sits in front of me, still licking and blocking Mum from view, so I tilt my head to look around him.

She frowns back and then peers down at her front. "Water, I was washing up. Did you hear what I just said?"

I nod, but she repeats it anyway.

"Stop screaming like that. The windows are open and everyone on the street can hear you. There are new renters moving in over there soon." She points toward the window. "They won't want to hear that."

"I know the window is there," I say, because it's true, I do.

She makes a stern face at me with a slight head shake, flared nostrils, and wide eyes, then scratches her head, sighing. "I know you do. But please, all that noise—I thought we agreed you'd stop getting so angry at your games. The neighbors will think there's a murderer in the house . . ."

I grind my back teeth together. "A murderer?"

Her eyes widen even farther. "Well, no, not really, of course, because that wouldn't happen. All I'm saying is that you can't keep screaming like that over a stupid game."

I wonder if murderers break into houses. I look behind Mum into the hallway, but I only see white walls and wooden floorboards and Dennis flopped on his back, half in and half out of Ned's doorway—nothing else. No murderers. I wonder if there's a murderer in Ned's room. Dennis wouldn't know if there was; he's not alert like Kevin.

Mum enters my room, her fluffy dotted flip-flops slapping against the floor, and she sits, causing my bed to dip and my legs to roll into her. I shift away toward the wall and swivel back to face my computer screen, clicking restart on Map Five, ready to play again.

"My game isn't stupid."

Kevin hops over my body and lies down beside me, and then I feel Mum's warm hand on the back of my leg, giving it a gentle squish. "I know, I didn't mean it. Is that the *Doom Tunnels* one?"

I stiffen and take two deep breaths in through my nose. "No. It's called *Tunnels of Disaster and Doom*, and this is Map Five. How could you forget that?"

"I don't play it every day like you, and my brain is full up with other things."

"Like cleaning the house and driving us to school?"

"And cleaning other people's houses and doing all the things because Dad's away."

I tap the arrow keys on my keyboard and move my robot up the ladder, hopping from side to side, and then switch to first person so I can see the beams clearly. When I first played Map Five, I fell off here a few times, landing in the lava at the bottom of the tunnel, but my friend hillieshillies66 from India told me to go first person as it's easier to do. He was right. Ned says hillieshillies66 might be a girl, so I shouldn't presume he's a boy, and that I shouldn't be making online friends with people I don't know. I'm not sure why; it's not like they're real friends.

"So you had a good day at school, then?"

"Yep," I answer as my robot somersaults off the beams and onto the sliding platforms.

"Did you play with anyone?"

"No."

"Talk to anyone?"

"Jared."

"The rugby boy?"

I press the down and side arrows at the same time, and my robot ducks and crawls under the fallen beams and then leaps over the next, then crawls and then leaps. I like this bit of Map Five the best.

"Jared plays rugby, right?"

"At school and for a club too. And he's the fastest boy in school and he's on my relay team."

"That's great. So is he your friend?" I feel pressure on my skin where Mum's touching me, so I shake my leg until she moves her hand.

"No. He doesn't want to play with me, but we run in the same group in PE, so he might be my friend if I can run faster and we make districts, or if I complete this map, or if I win a trophy at PAWS."

My tummy swishes when I say my plan out loud.

"But he's still nice to you, isn't he?"

I haven't seen Jared online yet, but when I do, I'm going to message him and finish telling him properly about how far I got in Map Five. He might tell me how to complete it.

Mum is still talking about people at school being nice to me, but then Kevin sneezes and jolts my arm and I hit the wrong arrow. My robot topples off the ladder and splashes into the orange lava, gray smoke puffing above it, and the word FAILED flashes across the screen.

"Agh, Kevin!" I yell, and stare at him. His big brown eyes stare back into mine through tufts of curly white fur and then he shoves his head forward and licks my face again, tail wagging.

"He's just a dog, Alex, he doesn't mean it," Mum says, and she stands, the bed springing back up with a pop. "And besides, dinner will be ready in five minutes, so you have to get off now anyway."

"Seriously?" I turn and watch her exit my bedroom, leaving the door open. Kevin doesn't follow her, just keeps licking my face.

"Yes, so switch that off now. You've been on it for over an hour." Mum's voice disappears down the hallway.

"I *seriously* can't believe this." I sit up on my bed and grab my pug pillow, squishing it tight to my chest. My eyes slide back to the flashing FAILED and I screw up my face. "I wanted to complete Map Five today. Now Jared definitely won't want to be my friend tomorrow."

Kevin lies across my lap, head resting on my thigh. I pat his head, his curls bouncing back up each time, and his tail wags slowly from side to side.

"Are you ready for PAWS on Saturday, Kevin?" His brown eyes rise to meet mine, and he huffs. "We need to win a trophy. Jared has medals and trophies from playing rugby, and Ella B. from dancing, and Cynthia S. from break dancing—they showed them to the class on Superstar Friday—and they all have lots of friends."

Kevin moves his head and looks over toward my desk, which is covered in dog figurines and framed photos and 3-D crystal dog puzzles. My underwater puppy calendar hangs on the wall above it, surrounded by sketches of Kevin and Dennis. Light, distant voices and the high-pitched squeaks of lorikeets stream in through the window along with a breeze, which flaps the calendar pages slightly.

I can see the four black permanent marker circles I made around November 12.

The day PAWS comes to Jessops Lake.

I bury my hand in Kevin's thick fur and look from November 12 to the word FAILED, still flashing on my computer screen.

I can't do Map Five, so if my legs don't get faster, a trophy is my last chance.

CHAPTER FOUR

I swipe another piece of buttered bread from the bowl and smear it through the delicious lasagna on my plate. I love lasagna. I love all soft food. Hard and crunchy foods make too much noise inside my head, so Mum doesn't give them to me anymore. Kevin sits between me and Mum, and his snout nudges the side of my leg, so I pat his head. He wants food but I'm not allowed to feed him at the table, even though I always see Ned throwing bits of food under the table to Dennis.

I glance over as Ned's voice rises. He's hunched over his plate, still wearing his white school shirt, but not the tie. I notice a blob of red on the front of his shirt. Lasagna. I want to say it aloud, point to it, tell them both that it's there. I open my mouth to speak but Mum speaks instead, and I stop my words because everyone is rude to me when I interrupt conversations.

"I won't be able to come and pick you up, Ned, so no, you can't go." Mum sips from her sweating glass of lemonade and wipes her damp forehead with the back of her hand, even though the ceiling fan is spinning above us.

"So I don't get to go. Brilliant," Ned says, his face frowny and angry.

"Ned, please."

"No, it's not fair."

"We all have to make sacrifices while Dad's away."

"Dad could get a job nearer. He doesn't have to work in the mines."

"Yes, he does!"

I jolt, Mum's raised voice exploding through my ears and into my brain. My heart thuds, and sweat springs from all my pores. I grip the edge of the table tightly. Kevin stands on his back legs and puts his front paws on my thigh, snuffling into my arm.

"Mum, why did you shout so rudely?" I whisper, sitting back against the wooden slats of my chair. "It made me jump."

Mum sighs and wrinkles her brow at me. "Sorry, sweetie," she says, her voice gentler this time. She pats my hand. I loosen my grip on the table, my muscles relaxing, and then look over at Ned. He stares down at his plate and swirls the last forkful of lasagna around it like he's sweeping the patio in the backyard. His cheeks are red.

"Ned, you know Dad isn't away forever, and I'm sorry it means you miss out on going out with your friends after school. I am giving up a lot at the moment too. I'd like to have some friend time myself right now, you know." Mum presses a finger into her forehead and then picks up her knife and fork. She sighs again. I think that might be the tenth one today, but I haven't been counting, so I'm not sure. "Are you angry because the new girl is going?" she adds.

Ned growls, making a mean face at Mum, then shoves the final bite of lasagna into his mouth. He stands with a huff, dumps his plate on the kitchen counter, and stomps out of the room.

"Who's the new girl?" I ask.

"And you can shut up too!" Ned yells over his shoulder.

I watch until he disappears around the corner and clench my fists until I hear his bedroom door slam, followed by the sound of a rapper's voice and loud drumbeats.

"Guess we said the wrong things." Mum sends a close-lipped smile my way.

"Can I take Kevin out into the yard again?" I ask, tearing the last piece of bread from the crust and cramming it into my mouth.

Mum smiles properly now. "What do you say?"

"Pees," I force out through the bread.

Mum grimaces but then nods. "Okay, but stay off the road, and come in before it gets dark."

I nod and stand, grab my plate, and place it on the counter next to Ned's. Once I've swallowed the bread, I click my fingers twice at Kevin, who trots beside me over to the bookshelf by the dining table.

"Is the book here?" I ask.

"Which one?"

"The one you told me about?"

Mum sighs. "I don't remember that conversation."

I grit my teeth. "The golden retriever book you told me about. Why don't you remember?"

Plates clatter and clink as Mum stacks them on top of one another. "Don't be rude to me, please. But yep, third shelf down on the right. Please be careful with it—it's very old."

I don't think I was rude to her.

I search where she said . . . *third shelf . . . on the right* . . . I hold up my hands to remember which is my right, and then I see the book and pull it out from between the others.

How to Look After Your Goldies.

The edges of the cover are folding outward and a bit cracked, and the pages look more yellow than

28

normal books. It must be old, because Mum said it was Grandad's when he was a boy and had a golden retriever. The dog on the front cover is so cute, the way it sits on the grass, a ball and a bone by its front paws. All its golden fur is brushed and looks so soft, and its black nose is raised in the air. Its pink collar has paw prints patterned all over it. "Aww," I say, and crouch beside Kevin, pointing to the book. "Look how cute she is." Kevin looks, shoves his nose into the picture, and makes a snorting sound.

"Ew," I say to Kevin, and stroke his head. "But not as cute as you."

I rest my head against his and pull him to my body. "Come on, Kevin, let's go learn some new stuff for the dog show."

* * *

A strong breeze, more of a wind, blows into the yard, and I breathe it in. I can always smell the ocean at this time of day. It's only a couple of minutes away by car, but we don't go often because even though I love playing in the waves and all the space, I don't like the sand.

It gets everywhere.

The palm fronds rustle high above me and birds flutter from tree to tree. I peer up at the sky, at the patches of blue among the white and gray clouds, and wonder if rain is coming.

Kevin whines and I look back at him and say, "Sit!" He stands five steps away, waiting. I lift my index finger, a dog treat concealed behind my other fingers, and then point down at him. He sits and I cheer, and then he gallops over and jumps up, paws scratching at my top.

"No." I push him down. "No, you have to stay sitting." Kevin sits by my feet, and a gust of wind raises his floppy ears and flaps my dark blue DOGS ARE COOL T-shirt. "We'll have to try again."

I walk backward five steps, smaller ones this time because I'm right near the edge of the driveway now and Mum told me not to go onto the road. I repeat the pointing action. "Sit!" But Kevin isn't looking at me anymore. His ears have rolled forward and his head is up, tilting. I hear a car engine behind me and turn to see a shiny blue Volkswagen round the corner.

"Come on, Kevin," I say, hooking a finger into his collar and scooting back up the driveway to the front door. I squat beside him, my eyes wide.

Cantering Court, where I live, is small—only

nine houses, all single level—and it's quiet because it's a cul-de-sac. I know Phil and Kuku at number eight next door; Sean and Jo at number six on the other side; Owen and his wife at number five; and Tanson, who is Ned's age but they're not friends, and his family at number four. I don't know the names of the people in numbers one, two, or three, but there are old people with two cats, more old people with no pets, and another family we never see. I also know everyone's cars.

This blue Volkswagen is not a car I've seen before. I like the color of it.

It stops beside number nine, its wheels scraping against the curb, and the engine shuts down, a faint ticking coming from the front. I wait, my arm draped over Kevin's back and my hand hugging his tummy. I'm still holding his blue collar in my other hand, my fingers buried in his soft fur. As I wait, focused on the car, I hear faint shouts and laughter from somewhere to my left—probably the loud family at the back of our house who had an argument with Dad once because they were cutting down trees without letting him know. I hear a siren, maybe a police car in the distance, and I smell food cooking, which I think might be a barbecue. I hear Ned's rap music drifting from his room at the back of the house, down the hallway, and out the front screen door to my ears.

And then I hear a pop and creak, and someone steps out of the blue Volkswagen. Another door opens, and then another. I see a girl first, as tall as Ned with white-blond hair tied back in a ponytail, and then a woman wearing sunglasses who has the same color hair, but hers is cut short. The other person is mostly hidden behind the car, but then they move toward the driveway of number nine.

It's a smaller person, also with light hair, wearing a Jessops Lake Primary School uniform. I dip my head, feel Kevin's fur against my cheek, and then the person turns, peering up and down my small quiet street.

It's the new kid from school, in grade six—a boy, I think, the one who sits on his own. His eyes reach me, and he raises a hand and waves. I know I should wave back, but instead I cling tighter to Kevin and watch the new kid, waiting for him to stop waving and looking at me.

His arm lowers and he turns, heading inside. His sister places a hand on his shoulder as their mum opens and then closes the black front door.

The new renters are here.

I wonder if the boy plays *OrbsWorld*.

TUESDAY, NOVEMBER 8

Four days to PAWS

CHAPTER FIVE

I adjust each of my pencils until they're all perfectly lined up against my ruler and the darkest, deepest scratch in the wooden desktop. They're like a rainbow, from black all the way to yellow, and it's beautiful. I don't have a white pencil. I will have to ask Ned if he has one he can give me after school. I won't use any of these colors other than black and gray and maybe blue, because that's my favorite color, but I still get them all out of my pencil case at the start of lessons.

Aqua is my favorite blue.

Ryan says I only like blue because Jared likes blue, but I don't think that's true because I've always liked blue. I wonder if the new kid with white hair likes blue.

A hand comes into view and taps my desk. I look up. It's Angel, who sits next to me. She smiles at me, strands of her jet-black hair strung across her cheeks, and whispers, "Ms. Westing called you for reading group." I stare at Angel's teeth and her pink lips, which look slippery because of all the lip balm she puts on, until the words make sense in my head, and then I glance around the room. Ms. Westing is smiling and beckoning me toward the Big B, which is a small area with beanbags and bookshelves at the back of our classroom.

I sigh and lower my chin and stare at my hands, which are squeezing my ruler. I don't want to do reading group. It's not that I don't like reading group or anything. It's just that today I want to finish my road map of Jessops Lake, like Jared and the other kids in my class are doing. If I do the same activities and work as they do, it'll give me more of a chance of Jared wanting to be my friend. Angel taps my desk again, and I move my eyes to the side until I see her map on her desk. It's the most awesome, coolest map out of anyone's in the whole class, because Angel is the best at art.

"I'll make sure no one moves your pencils," she says in a quiet voice.

Angel is nice to me. And she says I do brilliant art too.

I nod, then release my grip on my ruler and move my chair back silently. The other children chatter in quiet voices that make a low hum in the room as they work on their maps. As I weave through their chairs to the Big B, I see Ella's map, which is covered in red and gold, her favorite colors. Next to her is Jared's, all in pencil with sketches of balls and rugby players all over it. I don't think that's what he's meant to do, and I want to tell him, but I want more to turn back to my table, to Angel. But Ms. Westing says my name.

"Alex, we saved you the blue beanbag. Have a seat."

I do as she says because I'm a good boy and I always do as I'm told. I love the blue beanbag, and it shifts and molds around my butt and back as I sit. Ms. Westing hands me a piece of paper, folded in half, with a photo of a pizza on the front. I love pizza, but not the crusts, because they're too hard. I start to open the booklet.

"Oops, don't open it yet, Alex."

I glance up at her and she waggles her eyebrows up and down. I don't know what this means—it's not on my emoji chart at home.

"Right, we're all going to do silent reading first and then we're going to talk about what we've read. If you get stuck on any words, save them and we can talk about them at the end."

I turn my head to see the other four kids sitting around Ms. Westing: Chris, James, Joshua, and Matilda. I don't like sitting next to Matilda because she's loud. I understand that she has a disability, which means she can't always help it, but I can't help not liking her loud voice. We have reading group together four days a week—not Fridays—because we're all bad at reading. But Ms. Westing says we mustn't say that because how good you are at something isn't important, but how much fun you have doing it is. I don't know if that's right, because being good at *Orbs World* is important, and running fast is important too because it means our team might make districts. And winning a trophy at PAWS on Saturday is important, and to do that I need to have a dog that's good at things.

"Off you go then, Big Bees, open your booklets."

She always calls anyone who goes into the Big B "Big Bees."

I turn the page finally and take a look at the words.

Best Pizza Recipe Ever

Beneath the title is a list of ingredients, and underneath that is a method. Once I get to the bottom of the ingredients list, which has salami and pepperoni in it, my eyes don't see the words anymore. I hear the sounds of pencils scribbling on paper behind me and someone coughing and a chair scraping against the floor and Matilda breathing beside me and James scratching his skin. My chest feels a bit funny, and I grind my back teeth together, but I keep staring at the booklet and the lines of words. The words *salami* and *pepperoni* draw my eyes back up the page, but I'm supposed to read everything. I can see the others still reading out of the corner of my eye.

And then they're not reading anymore. They've all stopped and are looking at me.

"How are you getting on, Alex?" Ms. Westing asks.

I nod and close my booklet. "I'm finished," I say, and rest the booklet on my bent knees.

"Excellent. So, let's have some questions. At what temperature does the method tell you to cook the pizza in the oven?" She swivels on her green beanbag. "Chris?"

Chris adjusts his glasses, pushing them back up his nose. "Two hundred and twenty." He smiles, his lips all big and squishy-looking.

Ms. Westing nods and then looks at Matilda. "What do you think?"

Matilda slides her legs out and then draws them back in toward her body. She does this twice more before answering. "Two hundred and twenty degrees," she answers in her usual voice, where the words come out slower than everyone else's.

Ms. Westing smiles, and now she's facing me. "Alex?"

"Two hundred and twenty degrees," I answer, looking straight into her brown eyes like Chris did.

She nods and then moves on to James and finally Joshua. We all give the same answer, and Ms. Westing says it's correct. She asks some more questions about the method, asking us first in turn so it's not Chris all the time, and I listen carefully to what everyone else says so I can be right too.

But then it's my turn to be first.

"What do you think Matilda's favorite pizza topping is from the list, Alex?"

I frown at Ms. Westing because I have no idea. I don't know why she thinks I would know this. My cheeks and chest feel hot, even though the fan is spinning right above me.

"It's just for fun, so maybe have a guess," she adds.

I can't remember what was on the list besides only my favorites, so I say salami and pepperoni.

Matilda laughs. "No no no!" she shouts, squirming in her beanbag. And then she laughs louder, squealing and squawking.

I ram my hands over my ears. "Stop it," I say. "Stop shouting." But Matilda keeps laughing and saying no.

"Calm down, Matilda, calm down," Ms. Westing says, her voice stern and a bit rude.

I wait for ages, staring at my knees again until Ms. Westing taps me and I look up. She smiles and nods, and I take my hands off my ears but keep them close in case. It's quiet, apart from the sounds of Matilda's breathing.

"What do you say, Matilda?" my teacher asks.

"Sorry, Alex," Matilda says, but I don't look at her because I don't like her now. Apologizing is a nice thing to do, but everyone knows that part of my autism is having supersensitive hearing. Even Matilda. I used to wear my noise-canceling headphones in school, but I don't anymore. Jared and his friends don't need things like that, so I'm trying not to need mine.

"Okay, thank you. Alex?"

I shift my eyes up quickly to Ms. Westing. She smiles again, wrinkly skin and freckles stretching on her cheeks at in the corners of her eyes, and her curly hair bobs around her face.

"Matilda says her favorite pizza topping is tomato."

I look away again because I don't care. This time I fix my stare on the gray tiles on the floor and the dirty gray black lines that surround each one, and at my black shoes sitting side by side and flat in the center of one square tile. My laces are done up tight; I asked Mum to make sure because of what happened yesterday.

I do not like tomato.

"Everyone back to work," Ms. Westing says, the words flying over my head.

I turn, the beanbag rustling and getting stiff and hard in places. Lots of the other kids are looking over at us. My eyes find Jared. He has a grin on his face, then he whispers something in Ella's ear, and they both giggle and glance over toward the Big B.

I hate Matilda. She's made everyone stare, and now Jared and Ella are laughing at me. I should have stayed at my desk. I clench my fists tight like my laces. I hate school. I can't wait to go home. I'm going to play some *OrbsWorld* and try to finish Map Five, and then I'll practice tricks with Kevin before and after dinner, because now I need that trophy more than ever.

CHAPTER SIX

The bell rings. Finally, it's the end of the day and I get to go home.

I have not liked today.

It didn't get better after Matilda ruined everything and made Jared and Ella laugh at me. I grit my teeth as I think about it, but I ungrit them when I remember that I might get to play *OrbsWorld* if I tidy my room and that Kevin is waiting for me.

I push back my chair and grab my pencils one at a time, starting with yellow, as fast as my hands can go, and shove them into my pencil case. I don't care about the noise of everyone's chairs on the tiles or the loud talking or the way everyone charges behind me, because sometimes loud noises don't upset me. And right now I only care about getting back to my laptop and Kevin.

As I zip up my blue checked pencil case and put my English book away, Ms. Westing's shoes appear beside me. They're brown with small holes in them that are shaped like flowers. I know they're called pumps because Mum has a pair like them. I don't know why they're called pumps, though.

"Were you okay today, Alex?" she asks.

I nod. "Yes, thank you." The classroom door squeaks as it's opened and closed over and over again.

"You've been very quiet, and you didn't write as many words as you normally do." She crouches down so her eyes are at the same level as mine, even though she isn't much taller than me because I'm quite tall, one of the tallest in the class. Dad says that means my legs are longer and I should be able to run faster than everyone else, but so far that isn't true. I don't look at Ms. Westing's eyes, though. Instead, I keep staring at her pumps and how her long green dress brushes against the tops of them.

I don't know what to say.

"I know Matilda upset you today, but she did say sorry. Sometimes Matilda just needs extra help to understand other people's emotions." Her voice is softer now. I can't hear any noises in the classroom around us, but I can hear all the shouting and screaming of the kids outside, and I picture them all grabbing their bags and leaving the school. I wonder if Jared is still here. I might be able to tell him about *Tunnels of Disaster and Doom* Map Five. I didn't get a chance at recess or lunch because it rained so it was indoor play, but I always find that too loud so I went to the Harmony Learning Building instead with Miss Lucy, which is where kids who feel lonely or sad are allowed to go.

I nod again, still not sure what to say.

"Okay, honey. Well, I hope tomorrow you can show me some more of your amazing work, especially some of that fab artwork you do. It's Wednesday, don't forget."

Of course I won't forget. I love Wednesdays, because Wednesdays mean art and PE, where I get to train my legs to run as fast as Jared and his friends. Tomorrow is our last chance to make districts.

"And later this week we have the super special surprise assembly coming up, remember?"

Of course I do. I don't know why she's telling me things I already know about.

I look up at Ms. Westing's face and at her big grin that shows all her teeth. Her skin is even more wrinkly up close, which makes me think of Ned's dog, Dennis, but I don't say this because I once told Mikael J. that he looked like a Saint Bernard and his friends said I was mean and that made me upset, and then Mikael J. left Jessops Lake Primary School forever.

"That's right, on Friday there might be *something* about dogs . . ." Ms. Westing waggles her eyebrows again and I smile, because I think eyebrow waggling might be a good expression. "I know how much you love dogs, and I bet you're as excited as I am about the PAWS Dog Show on Saturday, right?"

"Yes," I say. "I'm entering my cockapoo, Kevin, into one of the contests, either tricks or obedience, because that's what he's best at, and then I can win a trophy."

"Excellent!" she says. "Well, make sure to practice. I can't wait to watch Kevin at the show and see what he can do."

I nod and smile and she winks and says good-bye, and I know this means I can turn and leave.

I push open the classroom door and find my bag—it's the only one left on the racks, but I know which one is mine anyway because it's in front of a label with my name on it and a pencil drawing of Kevin that I did. I grab my aqua water bottle from the box and start walking toward the gate. I hear someone close by mention PAWS and peek to my right at two boys. I don't know the boys—I think they're in grade five—but I listen. They're talking about the dog show. The one with black hair says he doesn't have a dog. The other boy, who has lighter brown hair than me, says he can't wait for the police dog performance, but then I don't hear any more because they turn right at the end of the path and I have to turn left.

I start thinking about what I'm going to do when I get home. I plan to do tricks with Kevin. We haven't practiced those yet, though he can already spin around on his back legs and roll over. I want to train him to lie on his back and then jump into the air, and in the golden retriever book it says—

"Did you cry today, Ally-Wally?"

My stomach becomes light and my breathing flutters in my chest. My eyes stay fixed on the ground, on the gravelly path, because that's Ryan's voice, and Ryan is nearly always mean to me. I keep moving my feet, staring at my shoes, the laces still in tight bows, listening to the noises of kids all around me and the cars out on the street. I want Ryan to go away.

"Was Matilda mean to you?" He makes a snorting sound.

I don't know how Ryan knows this because he's not even in 6W.

His shoes appear beside mine, the scuffing loud. I can also hear the sound of my heart beating in my ears. Ryan isn't wearing black shoes like he should be. His shoes are red with white laces and black stripes on the sides, and they're really clean.

"You're not allowed to wear shoes like that," I tell him.

"So what? None of your business," he replies. I see his hand fly at me and then it whacks against the hard edge of my cap.

I flinch as my cap flips off my head and lands on the path, and I want even more for Ryan to go away. I take a step to my right and bend to pick up my cap, heat and sweat all over my face. My eyes are burning and I can feel the tears that are about to come out. As I reach out, another hand appears, smaller than mine with lighter skin, and lifts my cap from the ground.

I open my mouth to tell Ryan to go away, but it's not Ryan. It's the new kid with the white hair who I saw at 9 Cantering Court yesterday.

"Leave him alone, Ryan, you bully," a voice says.

Both the new kid and I turn and see Angel with an older girl who's wearing a Jessops Lake Secondary School uniform like the one Ned wears, but with a black skirt instead of shorts. Angel has her hands on her hips.

"Oh, whatever," Ryan shouts at Angel, and then stomps away.

My eyes follow him as he keeps walking. I wonder if he'll turn around and come back, but he doesn't. Instead, he breaks into a run and disappears out the gate, his bag bouncing against his butt.

I wonder if Ryan might be faster than Jared.

"Are you okay, Alex?"

I look at Angel and nod and say, "Yes, thank you," and the older girl and Angel both give me the same smile and walk down the path toward the gate. Angel calls back over her shoulder that she'll see me tomorrow.

My body feels tight, like someone invisible is giving me a big painful hug, and my head is a bit confused. I turn back to the new kid, who is still holding my cap, and he moves it closer to me.

I take it from him, and before I can look away I notice that he has really blue eyes.

"Your eyes are blue," I say.

"Yeah," he answers, and he smiles, but only with one side of his mouth.

"I like blue. It's my favorite color," I add, then put my cap back on my head.

"That's cool. I like brown."

I frown. "I don't like brown."

The kid shrugs. "I do. It's the color of tree trunks and mud and fences and stuff. Your eyes are brown," he adds, squinting at me.

I look over at the road and at the cars parked along the side. Kids in Jessops Lake uniforms are still wandering up and down the path, some whizzing past on bikes.

"Is that your house I saw you at last night?" the boy asks.

I nod and glance up again at his blue eyes. They're not aqua, more like sky blue. I notice one of his feet at the bottom of my field of vision, kicking backward and forward, his knee bent a little, the *scrape, scrape* of the stones underneath.

"I'm going to be living at number nine. With my mum and sister. You can come over if you want."

I don't think I want to, because Mum says I shouldn't go to strangers' houses or to people's houses who aren't my friends, and I'm not friends with the new kid.

"My name's Derek," he says.

Nodding, I point to the gate. "I have to go because my mum and brother will be here soon."

"Okay, cool. My sister's waiting for me anyway. We catch the bus together."

I start walking and Derek walks beside me, close. I can hear the crunch of his footsteps and press my back teeth together.

"You like *Orbs World*?" he asks.

I look at him, my eyebrows rising a little. "How did you know?"

"I didn't," he says, doing his sideways smile again, his blue eyes all bright and wide. "*Orbs World* is my favorite game."

We exit the school gate, and there's a girl with really long white hair like Derek's waiting on the other side. It's the same girl I saw him with at 9 Cantering Court. She smiles at me, her lips pink and her skin shiny. She has a nice face.

"This is my sister," Derek says. "Mindy, this is . . ."

I stare at Derek, who stares at me.

"What's your name?" he asks.

"Alex."

"Alex," he repeats. "Alex, this is my sister, Mindy. Alex lives on the same road as us," he adds, looking up at his sister. Her eyes are exactly like Derek's.

"Well, hi, Alex." Her teeth are very white, like

her hair. She adjusts her bag on her back and pats Derek's shoulder. "We should go. The bus will be here in a sec." She walks ahead and gives me another smile.

"Okay, well, bye, Alex. See you tomorrow." Derek smiles too and follows his sister.

I watch them go, walking side by side and talking.

I wonder if Derek has completed *Tunnels of Disaster and Doom* Map Five.

CHAPTER SEVEN

I throw Kevin's ball high, and he jumps up to catch it but misses, his jaws closing onto air. He lands with a huff. The green tennis ball bounces behind him on the short grass, and he tries again to catch it, all four of his little paws launching him off the ground, but even though he can jump high for a small dog, he misses again. I shake my head and watch, my hands on my hips, as he scrambles after the ball. It bounces again and again until eventually it hits the brick wall below the kitchen window and he grabs it in his mouth.

"Kevin, that was rubbish," I say as he trots toward me, tail wagging and ears back. He drops the ball by my bare feet and I pick it up. It's all wet from his slobbery mouth. "Ew." I pinch the ball between the fingertips of my other hand and then wipe my wet palm against my school shorts, my nose wrinkling, and shake my head at Kevin. He's sitting right in front of me, staring at his ball.

"But you're bad at catching, Kevin, so what's the point of us practicing?" He cocks his head, ears pitched forward and dangling below his panting mouth. His tongue pokes out over his tiny, white, jagged teeth, and he looks like he's smiling even though Ned says dogs don't smile, it's just the way their faces look.

I'm not sure he's right.

I squat down and pat Kevin's head, his curls all soft. He licks my arm and then stands, nudging the ball with his nose. He looks up at me again, his big eyes browner than ever in the afternoon sunshine.

Derek would like Kevin's eyes. Maybe I can tell him about them tomorrow.

I swivel on my bare toes to face the road. My shoes are sitting side by side inside the front door, where I put them after taking them off on the way home, my feet hot and swollen from the humidity. I like having my feet bare when I'm at home.

Cantering Court is quiet, with only a few birds— magpies or crows, I think—calling to each other, the quiet yapping of a dog I haven't heard before, and voices shouting in the distance. It's probably kids playing in their yards like me, but I like to stay quiet, because being noisy makes people look at you.

The fourteen palm trees that grow in the front yards of Cantering Court reach high into the blue sky, which is so bright and seems to go on forever.

It's hot, but I stay in the shade of the trees like I'm always told to. Mum says that even though we're lucky to have such lovely brown skin, we can still burn, so we have to be careful. The sun beats down on the road, making it look like it has puddles on it, and the grass is scratchy under my feet. I shift them to make the feeling go away.

Not everyone is home from work yet, and the shiny blue Volkswagen isn't parked on the drive at number nine.

Derek said he and his sister were going to catch the bus, but no buses ever come up this road, so maybe he was wrong. When I was tidying my room, I kept looking out my bedroom window to see if a bus did come, but then Ned came in and shut my blinds and told me to stop being so nosy. I don't know why—I always look out my window at the neighbors and Ned has never said anything about that before. Then we both got in trouble because I was pulling the blinds up and Ned was pulling them down and Mum said we'd break them. "Pack it in, because I'm just about done with everything," she said. I don't know what she meant but I cried because I don't like it when Mum shouts.

Ned is weird and horrible. Mum says he's "growing up" and "a bit confused."

I don't think I'll be rude like him when I'm fourteen.

Kevin's wet nose nudges my hand, which is holding his ball, and I turn back and kiss him on the head, his curls tickling my cheeks and nose. Drool drips from his mouth and he pants loudly, *puff puff puff*, his face close to mine. I draw back and cough. "Ugh, your breath is smelly." Kevin keeps panting and I smile at him.

"Okay, we'll try a few more times," I say, scratching behind his ear, "but then we'll move on to tricks because you're better at tricks and that's how we'll win the trophy."

I stand up and tell Kevin to sit, but he already is, so I prepare to throw the ball. He shuts his mouth and ducks his head, which I know means he's getting ready to chase it. I throw it, higher and harder this time, but too far to the right. The ball goes straight over the fence and into my neighbor Phil's backyard.

"Oh no."

I clamp my back teeth together. Phil says Ned and I can go into his front yard to get our balls back anytime, but I can't get into his backyard because he has big locked wooden gates, and I know nobody's home because his white Toyota and his wife Kuku's silver Toyota aren't on the drive.

Kevin is staring at the fence, his tail not wagging anymore. He turns and looks at me and then at the fence, jerking his head back and forth. I grind my teeth a bit harder and he lets out a small bark.

"But I can't get it," I explain.

And then I remember that I have another ball inside, hidden in my closet. It's not mine, it's Ned's—I took it from him when I was ten after he stole my computer mouse and wouldn't give it back.

I smile, imagining Dad saying, "Good remembering," and Mum grinning.

"Right, wait here, Kevin," I say, but he's nibbling on his back leg now and not looking at me. I tiptoe-run up to the white-speckled porch, which looks silver in spots and burns the soles of my feet, and I swing open the screen door and rush to my bedroom. My blinds are pulled down, which means Ned must have come back in, so I pull the cord, sending them straight back up. They make a juddering, swishing sound as they climb and I pause, listening to make sure Ned doesn't come in and close them again.

I do *not* like it when he comes in my room.

Ned's door is shut, his NED'S MAN CAVE sign hanging lopsided, and I can't hear any noises coming from inside. He must have his big black headphones on.

Clinks and clatters of plates and the sound of Mum humming come from the kitchen, which means she's cooking—ham, egg, and chips tonight.

I'm safe.

I plop down on my bed and grab my notebook—the green robot one—and a pencil from the bedside table, and I open it to the half-finished sketch of Dennis. He's lying on his back, asleep, with his floppy white-and-brown face hanging off to the side, his gums and teeth exposed. I think it's Dennis's favorite position because he's always lying like that. He only gets up to greet people when they come in the front door—sometimes—and when there's food around. He doesn't even like to go out for a walk. But I love him anyway.

I think I love all dogs.

Adjusting the pencil in my fingers, I start lightly flicking the tip across Dennis's legs to show his fur. When I'm finished with that I shade some places darker to show the brown patches on his face. Some people say bulldogs are ugly, but that's mean because no dogs are ugly.

Angel told me to bring my notebook in and show her my new sketches, but I can only do that when I've used all the pages. She said she can't wait to see them.

It takes a few more minutes before I'm happy with this sketch of Dennis. I nibble the already chewed and dented end of the pencil as I admire the picture, looking to see if I can make any improvements.

I turn the page—only one more to fill and then it'll be done. I glance over to my bookshelves, at the four *Dog Hero* graphic novels Mum bought me that I haven't looked at yet and the forty-two other filled notebooks of sketches, which take up two and a half shelves.

I haven't always sketched my dogs. I used to draw *OrbsWorld* games and robots quite a lot, and also cars, but now I only draw dogs. Dennis is harder to draw than Kevin because I look at Kevin a lot more than Dennis, and when I shut my eyes I can picture him exactly as he is in real life.

My eyes open really wide.

I suddenly remember why I came into my bedroom. My insides feel like they're flipping over.

I forgot about Kevin.

"Kevin!"

I throw my notebook on the bed and hop up. I rip open my closet door and feel around at the back among all the jigsaw boxes and board games.

Got it. I pull out Ned's pink tennis ball.

Without shutting my closet door, I dart from my room, and charge back outside.

"Kevin!" I call, stepping onto the grass. "I have the other ball."

Kevin doesn't come, so I call him again, then wander around our small front yard looking for him. I even go through the side gate and into the narrow paved backyard where Dad cooks on the barbecue and Mum sits and reads, but Kevin's definitely not there.

I don't like it out here because there are often big spiders making webs.

My tummy swirls as I run back to the front yard, my eyes searching everywhere, my voice calling over and over for Kevin.

My heart is loud in my ears and I can't hear anything else apart from my shouts.

"Kevin!"

Again and again and again.

But Kevin doesn't come. He's gone.

CHAPTER EIGHT

The screen door bangs open and Mum runs out, the Guide Dogs tea towel I bought with my birthday money when I was nine flapping in her hand. It matches the colors of her blue shorts and white tank top.

"What on earth?" she says, her face frowning and sweaty, her hair pulled back into a ponytail. "What are you shouting about?"

"Kevin!" I shout. "I can't find Kevin." My voice doesn't sound like mine, and my cheeks and neck and chest hurt.

I stare up the street at all the houses, seeking out any sign of Kevin's white fur. All the sounds around me are unnaturally loud, hammering at my eardrums: Mum's flip-flops slapping the ground as she dashes back inside, the screen door squeaking open and then smashing closed, the squawking birds, and my booming heartbeat.

My chest squeezes and feels funny.

I can't lose Kevin. *Can't can't can't!*

I used to watch *Animal Rescue* on TV, about

dogs who go missing and wander the streets and get hit by cars or never find their owners, but I stopped because it made me too sad. I couldn't stop thinking about all those poor dogs.

That can't happen to Kevin.

But Kevin wears a blue collar with a paw print–shaped tag that has both the vet's and Mum's phone numbers engraved on it. Someone will call us if they find him.

The front door opens again, followed by the sound of footsteps coming closer, and then Mum's hand is on my shoulder, lightly resting there, and I don't shake it off. "Here, put your flip-flops on," she says softly. I see her toss my dark blue flip-flops to the ground, and I slide my feet, one by one, onto the soft fabric.

And then I hear Ned's voice. "Don't cry, Al, Kevin won't go far."

I nod, and Ned's fingertips wipe gently at my cheeks, and that's when I realize I've been crying. I take a shuddering breath and whisper, "I can't lose Kevin," which is the only thought in my head.

"Well, let's go find him, then," Ned replies. He pats my back, and all three of us, side by side like how I leave my shoes, walk forward, stepping out of the front yard and onto the stones of the road.

We turn left and pass Phil's yard, which has a white picket fence across the front. Behind the fence are flowering bushes and perfect green grass—much greener and brighter than ours, which is dusty and brown in patches. Mum says Phil and Kuku can have a yard like that because their children are all grown up and have left home, and neither Mum nor Dad is green-fingered, which means they aren't very good at growing plants.

Mum and Ned call for Kevin too, and we all look, craning our necks and ducking our heads to see over and between the fence slats and behind the bushes and on either side of the house.

Kevin isn't there.

I hear a sob come from my chest, and my bottom lip is quivering. The greens and browns and blues and the houses and the roofs and everything else are blurry behind my tears.

Ned pats my back again, and I snivel and sniff and wipe my eyes.

"It's okay, it's okay. Kevin won't go far because he loves you too much," Ned says.

I nod. Mum says Kevin was put on Earth just for me and that she's never seen a dog love a human so much. But now Kevin isn't here so maybe she's wrong.

The end of Cantering Court, where our house and Phil's and Derek's are, is shaped like a saucepan. We're following the curve of the curb, coming to the end of Phil's property. I hear the sounds of that yapping dog filter through the air again, a little louder this time. I remember hearing it as we practiced, Kevin's ears pricking forward and his tail freezing every time it distracted him.

We walk past number nine, the blue Volkswagen still not there. The gray driveway that takes up most of the front yard is glistening in the sunshine, as if there are a million jewels embedded in it. This house is the smallest on the street, single-story like all the others but with only the front door and one big window and no fence at the front.

"Call for him, Alex," Mum says. "He'll most likely respond to your voice."

But I don't call out, because I'm listening hard and I'm looking even harder. Kevin isn't anywhere out front of number nine, so I peer along the thin strip of gravel down the side of the house. I can just about see into the backyard. It's paved there, like my backyard.

The yapping dog is louder here and it's nonstop now. *Yap yap yap!* I think the dog is inside Derek's new house. As we walk past, I try to look inside the big window, but I don't see a dog in there, though it's hard to tell for sure because I can mainly just see our reflections. I try to look past Mum and Ned on either side of me, the same height as each other, and me in the middle, but it's no use.

My eyes stay fixed on the house, my ears blocking out Mum and Ned's shouts, focusing on the barking dog.

And then I hear a different bark. One I know.

Kevin.

"That's him!" I squeal. "I hear him!"

"Where? Where did it come from?" Mum asks, scuffing to a stop.

I listen again, harder, concentrating. *Yap yap yap!* But it's not Kevin's bark this time. I wander a few steps forward until I'm almost at the edge of number nine's yard, and this time I peer down the other side of the house, where white and brown gravel makes a narrow path all the way to the back.

And Kevin barks again.

"Kevin!" I shout. "KEVIN!"

My stomach swirls and my skin feels fizzy and my breathing gets fast.

Yap yap yap!

"Kevin, come here!"

And suddenly Kevin's head appears, peering

around the brick wall at the back of the house, ears forward. He barks once at me and then disappears again.

Yap yap yap!

"THERE HE IS!"

I'm about to run around the back of the house when I hear a car engine and freeze. I spin to face the top of Cantering Court, where I see the blue Volkswagen swing around the corner and crawl toward us.

Mum says something but her words don't go into my brain, and then she grabs my shoulder and pulls me back until we're all standing outside Phil's house again. My eyes don't leave the car. It pulls into the driveway very slowly, nothing like the way Dad parks his truck on ours. The Volkswagen rises with the curb, front wheels and then back wheels, and then it stops and the engine sputters as it cools down.

Three doors open at once. Out steps Mindy with her dark blue schoolbag in her arms, still wearing her school uniform. On the other side of the car are Derek and his mum. Mindy smiles at me and then peeks over at Ned, flicking her white hair back over one shoulder.

The car doors shut almost at the same time,

making a loud bang, which jolts me, and then Derek's mum comes around the back of the car, hooking a bag over her shoulder. It's a shiny bag that matches her high-heeled shoes and her black shirt and trousers.

Derek is behind her, still in his Jessops Lake uniform, and he lifts his hand and waves. "Hi, Alex," he says through his lopsided smile.

But I'm still listening to the *yap yap yap* inside the house, so I can't reply.

"Is everything okay?" Derek's mum says. Her accent isn't Australian.

Mum steps forward and Ned steps back, behind me.

"I'm so sorry," Mum starts, extending her right hand to Derek's mum. "I'm Kim, from number seven." She lets out a strange snort-laugh. "You must find it strange that we're all here outside your house." She snort-laughs again. "My son"—she puts her hand on my head, flattening down my hair—"Alex, has lost his dog and—"

"He's in your backyard!" I blurt, pointing at their house.

"He'll be saying hello to Vinnie, probably," Mindy says with a giggle, rolling her blue eyes and then peering over my head at Ned again.

67

Derek's mum takes Mum's hand and shakes it once. "Wilma," she says, then holds up a set of jingling keys. "Well, why don't you come inside and we can let the dogs meet properly," she says, smiling at me. Her smile is just like Derek's, all on one side. "But you must excuse the boxes. We are not done unpacking everything yet."

I glance at Derek. "You have a dog?"

"Yeah, Vinnie. He's a Jack Russell."

Jack Russells are good dogs, small and friendly and fun. I peer again at Derek's house, eager to see Kevin.

Wilma's heels click on the driveway to the front door, which she unlocks. Mindy follows, and so does Mum, but Ned stays behind me. Derek tilts his head toward his house.

"Come on," he says to me. "Vinnie will love meeting you."

I feel excited to meet Vinnie too. But most of all I'm excited to see Kevin.

CHAPTER NINE

Kevin's on the paved patio out the back. He leaps up at the glass kitchen doors from the outside, and Vinnie leaps up at the doors from the inside. Vinnie's still yapping, and it's high-pitched and fast: *yap yap yap*. It hurts my ears a bit as it echoes around the white kitchen, but I don't mind too much and it makes me smile and laugh. My smile gets even bigger as I watch Kevin. He's here, safe, and he looks funny, like he's on a trampoline.

"Alex!" Mum calls, but I keep watching Kevin, hands patting my thighs, *pat pat pat*.

"Alex!" Mum's voice is a bit louder this time, so I turn and see her standing with Wilma, Mindy, and Derek by the front door, beckoning me back. "Come and take off your shoes." She points at the floor next to her.

When I walked through the front door, I spotted Kevin straightaway and I ran, my flip-flops *flap flapp*ing on the white tiles.

I look down at my feet and then up at Wilma, afraid that she will tell me off. I don't like being told off.

"It's okay, Alex," Wilma says, striding into the kitchen, still in her heels. Mindy is right behind her, also still in her shoes. Wilma unhooks her bag from her shoulder and puts it on the black speckled counter. "We are not posh here." She turns to Mum and Ned. "Come through," she tells them, and they wander in, Ned behind Mum, his hands buried in his shorts pockets.

My tummy feels lighter now that I see Wilma and Mindy in their shoes. Something wet pokes at my shin, and I look down to see Vinnie sniffing me, his little white-and-brown tail sticking up and wagging from side to side. I crouch down and stroke his head. His fur isn't as soft as Kevin's; it feels prickly and smooth all at once. He's the same colors as Dennis, but smaller and skinnier, and his snout is pointier—and he has a proper long tail instead of a stubby one. Also, Vinnie is funny and is definitely smiling at me.

Derek squats beside me. Vinnie's tail wags even faster and he leaps into Derek's lap. Derek falls back onto his bottom and Vinnie climbs up onto his chest, licking and nibbling Derek's ears while he laughs and tells Vinnie to stop.

I like Vinnie.

I look back at Kevin, who's still outside but

sitting now, ears forward, head tilted, watching us with his tiny black nose pressed against the glass. "Awww," I say.

"Shall I let your dog inside?" Wilma asks, her hand already on the silver door handle.

I stand and nod. "Yes, please." She opens the door.

Kevin springs over the threshold and winds around my legs once, and then he and Vinnie immediately make a circle with their bodies, Kevin sniffing at Vinnie's bottom and Vinnie sniffing at Kevin's, and they move around and around until my eyes go dizzy and I have to look away.

"Oh, they are just the cutest together," Mindy says, sitting down on a stool at the kitchen counter and crossing her legs.

Mindy is right. Kevin and Vinnie are so cute, but now they've stopped circling and sniffing and instead they're swiping paws at each other and making growling sounds.

I step back and frown, holding on to the edge of the kitchen counter. "Are they fighting?" I ask.

"No, I think they're playing. I think they like each other," Wilma says, her blue eyes bright and smiley.

I study Vinnie and Kevin again as they scramble from side to side, low on their front legs, bottoms raised and tails wagging, and then they jump at each other, growling and pawing again. I think Wilma is right. Kevin looks like he's having fun, like he does when we play tug-of-war or when I throw his ball, so I smile again but don't let go of the counter, not yet.

Derek climbs to his feet and I notice that he's not wearing his Jessops Lake uniform anymore. "Would you like a drink, Alex?" he asks.

"When did you change your clothes?" I ask, my eyes growing wide when I see the big red *O* above the zigzagging *W* on his white T-shirt—the *OrbsWorld* logo.

"I like to change out of my uniform as soon as I get home." He shrugs and then points to the fridge. "Did you want a drink?"

I put a finger to my chin and think about my mouth and my throat. They feel dry and scratchy, so I nod. "Just water . . ."

"Please," Mum's voice adds.

"Please," I repeat.

"Coming right up!" Derek says. He skips past me and opens one of the glossy white cupboards.

"Good idea, Derek!" Wilma says, clapping her hands together, which makes me startle and grip the counter a bit harder. "We should have a cup of tea. Kim, do you have time?"

"I'd love one," Mum replies.

"Please sit. And Mindy? Would you like to offer your friend a drink?"

As Mum takes a seat at the breakfast bar, my eyes move from her to Derek, who is filling a glass with water from a tap in the door of the silver fridge, and then to Mindy, who hops down from her stool silently and wanders over to Ned. Ned is so quiet I forgot he was here, and his cheeks are redder than normal, but I don't think he's angry, which is usually when his cheeks go red.

Loud panting distracts me from my brother's strange expression, and soft fur rubs against my leg. I look down and stare into Kevin's eyes. His tail wags so fast it makes him all wiggly. I hold out my hand, which he nuzzles and licks, still looking up at me. I drop to my knees and kiss his head and close my eyes. "I love you," I whisper, my lips and nose buried in his white curls.

Mum and Wilma's voices mumble and there's a *shush*ing sound, which I think is a kettle. I open my eyes and straighten up.

Derek hands me the glass of water. He's holding Vinnie, who is tucked under his other arm. I can see Vinnie's tail wagging and he's panting just like Kevin.

"Want to come see my room?" Derek asks.

I look at Mum, not sure if Derek is still a stranger and maybe I should say no, but she meets my eyes and nods, her eyebrows raised. "But not for long," she says. "I'm halfway through cooking dinner."

I turn back to Derek. "Okay," I say, "but not for long, as Mum is halfway through cooking dinner."

Derek frowns a bit and then smiles, his lips more lopsided than normal. "Come on, then," he says, and leads the way.

My heart beats a little faster as I leave Mum and Ned in the kitchen. I grip my glass of water tighter, the coldness cooling my hot palm, and I focus on Mum's voice behind me, asking Wilma where she's from. Wilma answers, "Sweden," which is a town I don't think I've heard of. Then Derek and I are turning right and Mum's voice disappears. I switch my focus to Kevin, who is trotting in front of me, his claws clicking on the tiles gently. He's looking up and watching Vinnie's tail wag. Derek opens a door with his free hand, then puts Vinnie down and enters the room.

"Come in," Derek says, and so I do.

Derek's room isn't as big as mine but it's much better. It's the best room I have ever seen—I nearly drop my glass of water. I stand in the doorway, my eyes moving from wall to wall, from *Orbs World* posters to *OrbsWorld* drawings to an *OrbsWorld* clock to *OrbsWorld* pillows to a whole shelf above his bed filled with *OrbsWorld* toys. He has robots and ants and cars and dragons, and I want to look at all of them. And then there's another shelf, higher up, filled with trophies.

"Wow. You have so many trophies and so many *OrbsWorld* things," I say, my tummy twisting and my breathing speeding up a bit.

"I love *OrbsWorld*," he says, lying back on his red-and-white-striped bedspread, "and my dad works for the company that owns *OrbsWorld*, so he can get me all this cool stuff."

"That is awesome," I say. I glance at him on his bed; both Vinnie and Kevin lie next to him, Kevin watching me.

"Yeah, it's kind of cool, I guess," Derek answers, but he doesn't smile when he says it, which I don't understand. I wish Dad worked for the same company as Derek's dad so he could get *OrbsWorld* toys and posters for me.

I sit on the edge of the bed, still admiring his *OrbsWorld* things. "Have you played *Tunnels of Disaster and Doom*?" I ask.

"Yeah, that used to be one of my favorites, but I prefer to play *Skyscraper Escapades* now."

I turn back to Derek. Vinnie is now lying across his chest and trying to eat the label in the back of Derek's T-shirt, tail still wagging. "Have you completed Map Five and gotten the eighty million Orbsicles?"

"Yeah, that one's pretty hard—it took me ages to get past the ant platform."

"Yes!" I reply, spinning on my bottom, some water sloshing out of my glass and onto my leg. Kevin lifts his head and starts licking it off my skin. "I can't get past that platform. I keep getting forty million Orbsicles, but I want the jackpot so I can trade rations at the fair and then move on to Map Six so I can play with my . . . Jared." My chest flutters and I tap my teeth together.

"It's not that difficult once you know how," Derek answers.

I nod and chew the inside of my mouth, not sure if I should ask for his help.

"That Ryan kid is pretty mean," Derek says, and I nod again, but I don't want to talk about Ryan.

"I wish I could get past the ant platform," I say.

Derek narrows his eyes at me and shrugs. "I'll show you how when I get my computer back."

I don't know where his computer has gone but a smile spreads across my face, and then I gulp down all my water in one go and gasp when I'm finished.

Derek laughs as he twirls Vinnie's little white triangle-shaped ears with his index fingers. "Everyone was talking about the dog show at school today. Are you going?" Derek asks.

I nod. "I'm entering Kevin into one of the contests, probably obedience or tricks because that's what he's best at. What are your trophies for?" I point to his shelf.

Derek glances up to the high shelf and shrugs, which he does quite a lot and I'm not sure why. "For fishing. I used to go with my dad a lot."

I've never been fishing before but now Derek's face looks like the sad emoji on my chart, so I don't think I want to, even if you can win trophies for it.

Kevin's looking up at me with his brown eyes, so I place my hand on his soft ear, the softest part of his whole body, and try to touch his nose with mine. He licks my face before I can. I think Kevin might be the fastest licker ever.

I wonder if that is a contest at PAWS because Kevin would definitely win.

"Are you going?" I ask.

"Where?"

"To the PAWS Dog Show."

"I dunno. Maybe. Depends if we go to Dad's or not."

I chew the inside of my mouth a bit more, not really sure what Derek means because surely his dad lives at 9 Cantering Court too, but I don't know what to say about that. I glance back at Vinnie's cute face. "If you go, you should enter Vinnie into the contests as well because you could win a trophy—another one that makes you happy and makes you new friends at school."

Derek studies me, the sun beaming through his window and making his blue eyes look even more blue. He has a small line between his eyebrows. I look down at Kevin, who's resting his chin on my lap, because I don't recognize any visual clues in Derek's expression that can help me understand him. I'm not sure if he heard what I said and wonder if I should say it again. My brain is confused but I need Derek to understand, so I open my mouth and blurt: "I'm autistic."

I glance at him and he nods. "That's cool. Thanks for telling me."

Weird. I didn't expect him to say that, which makes me feel even more confused. I stand in silence for a second, patting my thighs gently, trying to make my brain come up with more words, something better to say.

"Want to look at my *OrbsWorld* figures?" Derek asks.

I nod, and while Vinnie and Kevin sleep on Derek's bed, their heads dangling over the edge side by side, Derek spends lots of minutes showing me each of his toys and models, letting me hold each one. Then I hear Wilma calling us and we go back into the kitchen, which now smells of tea.

"Did you boys have fun?" Wilma asks.

"Yeah. Alex says I should enter Vinnie into the dog show on Saturday. Can we go?" Derek asks his mum, who wraps one of her long, pale arms around his shoulder and pulls him into her side for a hug.

"Let's hope so," she says, her voice gentle.

Mum thanks Wilma for the tea and tells her she'll pop over tomorrow with "a bottle of cleaning product that should get the stain out of the shower no problem," and then they kiss each other on the cheek and we head toward the front door. I'm not sure why Mum kissed a stranger; normally she only kisses Dad, me, Ned, and her friend Mags, though Mags now lives in South Australia, so Mum doesn't see her much anymore.

"And I will send Ned home soon, after they've finished the homework," Wilma says, winking at me.

I have no idea what this wink means, just like I don't when Ms. Westing winks, and I wonder where Ned is but guess he's with Mindy, maybe in her bedroom, as she isn't in the kitchen either.

I wonder if Mindy likes *Fight Forest* and rap music.

We step outside, the aroma of seawater and the hot air instantly swarming me, along with the sounds of people talking across the road and birds in the palm trees and the buzzing of a lawnmower somewhere nearby.

"Bye, Alex," Derek says, standing in the doorway with his mum.

"Bye, Derek."

Mum waves to Wilma as we walk away and I hear her sigh, and then she lightly strokes my head. Tomorrow I will have to spend more time training Kevin, but maybe in the hallway or kitchen at home. I wonder if I will see Derek at school tomorrow. Maybe he'll tell me how to complete *Tunnels of Disaster and Doom* Map Five at lunch.

I smile and look down at Kevin, who trots along by my feet. I can't wait to go to school tomorrow because Wednesday means PE and relays.

WEDNESDAY, NOVEMBER 9

Three days to PAWS

CHAPTER TEN

Kevin sits beside me, his nose resting on my right thigh as I eat my porridge. A lumpy splodge topples off my spoon and down my aqua pajamas, and I dab at it with the napkin Mum left me because she knows I always spill my breakfast. That's why I don't put on my Jessops Lake uniform until after I've finished. Kevin's front paws land on my lap as he stretches up to help me clean off the porridge with his tongue. I giggle and pat his head, then go back to eating.

Mum is in the shower. If I concentrate, I can hear the water rushing through the pipes above the ceiling. I swing my legs under the chair, my bare toes brushing the floor, and look at the pictures on the "Teach Him to Speak" page in *How to Look After Your Goldies*, which is open on the table next to my bowl. There are step-by-step guides with short instructions beside each hand-drawn picture. I've now read through them five times—this is my sixth—skipping over the words I don't know.

I glance down at Kevin, who's still half standing on my lap, watching my spoon move from the bowl to my mouth and back again.

If I can teach Kevin to bark on command, I will have trained him to do seven tricks: bark, sit, give paw, lie down, roll over, spin on his back legs, and stay . . . sometimes. It could be enough to win the trophy. He's not good at catching his ball, though he does bring it back most of the time, so we could use fetch as one of our tricks, which makes eight.

I swallow my last mouthful and leave my spoon in the blue bowl, the handle on the right. "When I get home from school, we'll do speak commands," I tell Kevin. "And then we need to practice some more catching and fetching." I scrunch my lips from right to left and run my hands up and down Kevin's front legs, ruffling his fur up and then smoothing it back down, feeling his bones under the thick curls. He licks my cheek. "I don't really know the difference between tricks and obedience," I add, "but I think they're basically the same, so we can do all the same things in both contests."

Footsteps pad around the corner and Ned enters the kitchen, Dennis lolloping behind him. Ned's hair is gelled perfectly to one side and his tie is neatly tied, and he smells different, a smell

I haven't smelled before. It's strong and travels up my nose too fast, and I cough. "What's that smell?" I say, covering my nose and coughing again. Kevin sneezes.

Ned doesn't respond and I see he has his earbuds in, the wire attached to his phone in his pocket. He's stirring chocolate powder into a glass of milk, the spoon clinking lightly against the sides, and I wonder why he's ready for school already. Normally Mum and I end up waiting at the door for him, Mum's voice getting louder and louder each time she calls until she stomps up the hall to get him.

My brain tells me it's because he's looking forward to seeing Mindy at school. I wonder if Mindy is also the new girl Mum mentioned at dinner on Monday, which made Ned growl. I think I might be right, but I don't say anything because I don't want Ned to growl at me too.

He wanders over to the table and sits opposite me with his chocolate milk and a bar of chocolate, and I wonder if Derek likes chocolate. Dennis disappears under the table.

There aren't many blue foods.

"Mum says you can't have chocolate for breakfast," I say, pointing to the purple wrapper.

Ned looks over at me and takes out one of his earbuds. "All right, Alex," he says. "Did you say something?"

My finger is still pointing at the chocolate bar in his hand, but before I can repeat what I said, Ned unwraps it and takes a huge bite, almost half the bar, smiling at me as he chews. My eyes are wide and I glance at the corner of the room, listening carefully. The water isn't *shush*ing through the pipes anymore, which means Mum is out of the shower and will come into the kitchen soon, and then she will tell Ned off and might shout again, because she shouts so much more now that Dad is working away. My tummy twists and I clench my fists because I don't want to hear any shouting. I stare at Ned, and he shoves the second half of the chocolate bar in his mouth and screws the wrapper up, the plastic crinkling loudly, and jams it in his pocket.

I continue to stare at him as he swallows the chocolate and then gulps down his chocolate milk. He finishes it and then smiles at me and winks. Another wink.

"Why did you wink at me?" I ask. I know Ned will tell me why because he came to the Be Aware classes with me and Mum, so he knows sometimes I need help understanding people's expressions.

He shrugs. "I dunno," he says. "I suppose because I thought it might make you laugh. And also to tell you not to tell Mum, okay?"

"Tell Mum what?" I ask, frowning, still not sure what the wink meant and wondering if Ms. Westing and Wilma were trying to make me laugh as well.

"That's the way," he replies, winking again.

My heart beats a bit faster. I want to shout at Ned because he didn't answer my question and because of all the winking he keeps doing and because no one has ever told me about winking before, and my face is growing hot, but then Kevin is on my lap, all of him, and he has his front paws on my shoulders and he's licking my face. I hold his sides, leaning my head back until it bumps into the wooden back of the chair, and I move it from side to side to escape his wet tongue lapping at my cheeks, but he doesn't stop. "Kevin," I say, moving my hands to his mouth. "Stop licking!" But he doesn't. He just keeps on licking, now on the palms of my hands and my fingers.

I hear Ned laugh. "Good boy, Kevin," he says. "Keep licking him."

"No more, you can stop now, Kevin," I say, and he does stop, hopping off my lap and landing silently just as Mum flip-flops around the corner, bringing with her the smell of flowers, which I know is from the shower gel Dad bought for her birthday last month, two days before he had to go work in the mines.

"Morning, you two," she says, pouring herself a glass of orange juice from the fridge.

I nod and Ned says hello, and then he turns to me and pats the golden retriever book. "How's the training going?" he asks.

I nod again. "I need to teach Kevin to speak on command and then we'll have seven tricks, or maybe eight tricks if he can catch and fetch a ball, but I'm not sure about that one yet, but if we show them all I think that will be enough."

"Enough for what?" Mum asks, putting fruit into our lunchboxes.

"To win the trophy," I say. "How do you not remember that?"

"Okay, Alex, sorry, I don't remember you telling me." She shakes her head, but I wasn't rude to her, so I don't know why she's cross with me. "You might not win the trophy, though—you have to prepare for that," she adds, folding her arms across her pink top and leaning back against the wooden counter.

I frown. "Of course we will win the trophy," I reply. "Kevin is the best dog and we've been practicing all our tricks." I give Kevin a pat.

"I know, sweetie," she says, "but you have to remember that there will be other dogs there whose owners take this kind of thing very seriously."

"Yeah, like that guy we saw at the dog park a few weeks ago with the Dalmatian. Remember?" Ned says.

I do remember. I sat on the bench next to Mum with Kevin by my feet, watching the man with the bald head teaching his dog to flip and walk backward and jump into his arms and over the hurdles and up the ramp. Kevin only ever pees on those, even though I try to make him do all the things he should do.

I stare at my empty bowl, my breath coming faster. I feel Kevin rest his chin on my leg, and I clench my fists tighter and tighter until my knuckles hurt. I meet Kevin's brown eyes and I want to cry because I love him but he can't do any of *those* tricks, and if the bald man and his Dalmatian turn up to the dog show we will never beat him and win the trophy.

"Come on, Alex," Ned says. "You never actually thought you'd win a trophy at PAWS, did you?"

"Ned," Mum says, her voice stern, and now a tear is falling down my cheek because I *did* think we could win a trophy but now I don't know.

"What?" Ned answers.

"You know what—why did you have to say that?" Mum keeps putting things in our lunchboxes, the banging of cupboard doors and the rustling of tinfoil and the snap of the lids sealing all making my tears fall faster.

"Sorry, Alex." Ned stands, and I'm angry with him, and then I notice the purple wrapper poking out of his pocket.

"Ned ate a chocolate bar for breakfast and he's gelled his hair and is ready early because he wants to see Mindy at school." The words tumble out, broken by sniffs and shudders as I catch my breath.

"Oh, nice one, you idiot," he says, banging his hand down on the table in front of me, which makes the spoon clink in my bowl.

"NED!"

I startle and scream, leaping up from the chair and running to my bedroom, my ears buzzing as the air whooshes past. I rush inside my room, Kevin right on my heels, and I close the bedroom door and climb under my blankets, clapping my hands over my ears. I cry and scream until I can't breathe so I can't hear Mum and Ned arguing, and then I poke my head out and gasp in big gulps of air. Kevin's right beside me but he doesn't lick me, and after I've wiped the tears from my eyes I see that his ears are far back and his tail isn't wagging and he's whimpering. I throw my arms around his neck and hug him tight, and he continues to whimper into my ear until I let him go, and then he starts licking me. I lie back and rest my head on my pug pillow.

There's a *knock knock* at my door and it opens just a crack, Mum's red face poking through the gap. "Baby," she says, a sad smile on her face. "Can I come in?"

I don't nod or say anything but she comes in anyway and sits on the bed next to me. Kevin stops licking me so he can lick Mum, and she smiles and kisses his nose. I see a tear roll down her cheek and she sniffles, which makes Kevin lick her some more.

"Sorry about all that," she says after a few seconds. "Ned's finding it all a bit hard without Dad around ... well, I am too." She closes her eyes and takes a deep breath. "Your brother is a good boy, really."

I stare at my bookshelf, at the spines of all my notebooks squished next to each other. I don't know why everyone is finding it hard without Dad because all the same things happen every day, but I wish he'd come back because Ned isn't a good boy at the moment, though he did used to be. If that's because Dad is away, then he needs to come home quickly.

"Anyway, you probably should try not to tell on Ned like you did, and definitely don't mention Mindy again . . ." She glances over her shoulder at my open bedroom door. "I think Ned likes her," she whispers.

I nod and she leans forward, gently brushing her hand against my cheeks. I let her because sometimes Mum's hands feel nice and it helps me to calm down when my beaker is too full and spills over.

"Right, let's get ready for school," she says, smiling, her lips parting to show her perfect straight teeth. "It's Wednesday, your favorite day."

My chest and insides feel lighter, and I sit up as she kisses my forehead and leaves the room, closing the door behind her, and then I stand and get dressed in my school uniform. Kevin flops down on my pug pillow in my place, and I drop my pajamas into a pile in the corner.

I hate school so much, but Wednesday means art and PE, which means I get to train my legs to run as fast as Jared's and help us make districts. If the man with the bald head and his Dalmatian go to PAWS, then today's relay race is more important than ever.

Kevin stares at me and sits up, offering me his paw, and I take it and squeeze it gently, rubbing my thumb up and down his toes. Another week is nearly over, which means graduation is nearly here, which means secondary school is nearly here too, and all this means I don't have much time left to make a real friend who wants to play with me.

CHAPTER ELEVEN

I clutch my green robot notebook in both hands, my pencil case balanced on top as my class makes its way to the art room. I walk next to Joshua, and Angel is two rows behind me. I turn and look at her and she gives me a wave, her fingers moving one at a time.

I can't wait to show her all the drawings in the notebook. I added the final one before I fell asleep last night, with only my blue star lamp shining in my dark room. I hope she likes the sketches, especially the last one because it's the best one I've ever done. I want to open my book now and look at it, but I don't because I don't want anyone else to see inside. Only Angel, because she's nice to me, even though she's not my friend—she only plays with Deidre and Linda.

All the other kids in the class are walking quietly in pairs behind me, their feet clomping and skidding and scuffing on the stones. Ms. Frisp, the art teacher, leads the way right in front of me, her black boots that come up to her knees barely making a sound even though her steps are fast. Ms. Frisp is always quiet and likes her classes to be quiet, and she's strict. When she does speak, her voice is loud and sharp and makes me think of a knife, so everyone behaves themselves, which is another reason I like art the best.

We turn the corner into A block and follow Ms. Frisp down the steep steps with all the tall trees whose long branches arch over us, making a green-and-brown roof that sways and rustles and keeps the heat and brightness off my hot skin.

Ms. Frisp opens the art room door and we file inside the hut, taking our seats in near silence, only the odd whisper and murmur here and there, which sounds a little like the leaves outside moving in the wind. I sit in my chair at the side of the room at table one, with Angel beside me and Wu and Isaac opposite.

"Good morning, 6W," Ms. Frisp says, her words silencing the final sounds as everyone settles. I place my pencil case on the white tabletop, the zipper in line with the edge, and then rest my palms flat on top of the notebook on my lap, trying my hardest to keep my breathing calm and listen to Ms. Frisp and not open it and look at the last sketch of Kevin.

"We're going to finish our self-portraits today,

so starting with table one, please fetch your trays and get to work."

I stare at my notebook, my fingers tracing the edge of the robot—his square head and rectangular arms and legs and his square feet. It's not an *OrbsWorld* robot, but it's the best Dad could find for me before he went away. I wish my book was blue and the robot was from *OrbsWorld* and that Dad worked for the same company as Derek's dad, but Mum says we can't always have everything we want when we want it, and that sometimes we have to find the good in what we've got. I think I understand what she means but I still wish and hope.

I grab my tray and head back to my table.

"Mr. Freeman," Ms. Frisp barks from her desk, and I wonder who she's speaking to. I'm just about to sit down when Ms. Frisp says "Mr. Freeman" again, and I look up and see that she's staring at me.

"Yes, you, Alex Freeman."

My heart beats fast and my ears whoosh, and I can see the other children all looking at me in the edges of my vision.

"Come here, please," Ms. Frisp says, and beckons me with a long finger, but I don't move because the room suddenly gets very small and everyone's faces are too close and I think some people are laughing at me or maybe just coughing.

I swallow and start walking toward Ms. Frisp's desk, but I don't look at her, only her desk and the open laptop and the pot of pencils and the attendance book and other papers and the small model piano with a cat sitting on top of it. Most of the teachers at school know that I'm autistic and can't be called up to the front of the class like this because I get so anxious. But maybe Ms. Frisp doesn't know. Maybe someone needs to tell her.

"Table two, carry on," Ms. Frisp says as I stop and stand on the other side of her desk, the cat now closer and clearer. I can see its ginger and white stripes and black eyes and pointed ears. I don't like cats as much as dogs, and Mum is allergic to cats, so we can never have one anyway.

"May I?" Ms. Frisp asks, and I see her bony arm and fingers—which make me think of a greyhound—stretch out in front of me and point at my chest. I don't know what she means, but then I look down and remember that I have my robot notebook, and my eyes dart up to her face.

"Yes, may I take a look?" she asks, and I study her expression quickly before looking away. She isn't smiling but she also doesn't look angry, but I don't want to give her my notebook because I brought it here to show Angel and I've only ever shown Angel my sketches. But I have to do as I'm told because I'm always a good boy, so I pull it away from my chest and hold it out to her.

She gently takes it from me and my hands shake as I watch her lower it to her desk, placing it down at an odd angle in front of the laptop, and my breathing gets faster and faster.

"Don't worry, Mr. Freeman, I will return it to you at the end of class, I promise." Her long pink fingernails, the same pink as Mum's top, rest on top of the robot's face. "You may go work on your portrait."

I turn and watch my shoes and their tight laces as I walk back toward table one. I sit in my seat and see my tray with my half-finished portrait and the chalks and paints and materials inside right in the middle of the tabletop, in line with my pencil case.

"It's okay, Alex," I hear Angel whisper. "You'll get the book back and then you can show me, 'kay?"

I think I nod but I'm not sure, and I keep staring at my tray. The clanking of trays on tables and the sliding of chairs and the scratching of pencils and brushes and the *snip snip* of scissors take over all my thoughts, but I don't scream or cry because I can't, not here and not now, so I just stare, clenching my back teeth so hard my head starts to hurt.

I have never been in trouble at school ever but today I think I am and I don't know why, because all I did was bring my notebook to show Angel and I wasn't talking or being naughty like some of the other boys have been before. I hate Ms. Frisp.

I take my portrait from my tray and stick on more furry material for my hair and tissue paper for my irises, but I don't do as much as I normally would and I don't enjoy it as much as I normally do because I can't stop thinking about my notebook. Then Ms. Frisp calls out again, telling us to clean up. I put my hands over my ears as the noise level in the classroom rises and everyone does what they're told, getting ready to leave the art room and head to PE. Angel takes my tray along with hers but her movements are blurry, and it's not until she taps on the table in front of me and then on my pencil case that I take my hands off my ears and stand up and start walking to the door with everyone else.

"Mr. Freeman," Ms. Frisp calls, and this time I go over to her desk straightaway, my breaths huffing all fast and hot through my nostrils. I hold out my hand but she doesn't give me my notebook.

"Angel, please tell your next teacher that Mr. Freeman will be along soon."

I stare at Ms. Frisp's wrinkled hand holding my notebook as I hear Angel say, "Yes, Ms. Frisp," and I wait, because this has never happened before—not with a teacher, anyway. I'm not sure how to take my book from Ms. Frisp because Mum and Dad always tell me not to snatch, and even Kevin has to take things gently from my hand.

"You have some very good drawings in there, Mr. Freeman," Ms. Frisp says, but I keep staring at her hand. "I knew you were good at art, but these are very special sketches. Very special."

I nod this time, a new light feeling in my tummy because it makes me happy to hear that Ms. Frisp likes my drawings of Dennis and Kevin. Ms. Frisp used to own an art gallery in London in England and knows a lot about art and judges lots of art competitions.

"Are you going to the PAWS show on Saturday?" she asks, and when I nod again I glance up at her face. Ms. Frisp is much older than Mum and her face isn't very nice, but her eyes are a mixture of gray and blue and I like them. "That's good to hear," she says.

I wait. My book is still in her hand, and I wonder why she isn't giving it to me or saying anything else. The classroom is silent behind me. Everyone will be at PE now, and if I'm late I might not get there in time to run fast in the relay.

This is not how today is supposed to go. A big ball of anger is growing in my tummy now.

"Alex," Ms. Frisp says, "I wonder if I might keep hold of your book until Friday, please. If that's okay with you, of course."

I pause at her words, which she says in a voice that's softer than I've ever heard her use before, and I frown and think. I'm not sure if I want to leave my book with Ms. Frisp, but if I do what she asks I might be able to make it to PE in time.

"I promise to return it to Ms. Westing on Friday to give back to you. I never break my promises, Alex."

And she did say please.

So I nod and Ms. Frisp places the book back down on her desk.

"Thank you, Mr. Freeman," she says, giving me a tight smile. "You may go."

I turn and stride to the classroom door, my pencil case gripped tight in one hand as I prepare to break into a run. I have to make it to PE in time because this is our group's last chance to make districts.

"Oh, and Mr. Freeman, your portrait is wonderful too, and you will have next lesson to finish it."

I nod once, rip open the door, and run as fast as my legs will carry me to my classroom in D block. I put my pencil case in my tray and shove my cap on my head, and then I charge back out into the heat and the sunshine and sprint all the way to the fields.

I have to make this day work out like I planned.

CHAPTER TWELVE

Birds chirp and squawk as I fly through the shaded area and past classrooms on my way to the fields. My shoes crunch on the gravel, and I hear my breaths loud in my ears. I'm not allowed to run on concrete, especially this fast, but everyone is in classes, and I'm so late for PE and need to get to the fields right now.

But my thigh suddenly hurts and I cry out and have to slow down. To stop it from hurting so bad, I only put my toes on the ground instead of my whole right foot and carry on as fast as I can. I can see the green of the fields opening out ahead, and all the kids from 6W and 6P are there already with Mr. James, who's calling out instructions like "Get in your groups" and "Decide who'll go first" and "Come grab a baton."

I hobble across the bridge that runs over the small ditch where Ryan always says there are big snakes. I've never seen a snake in there, but we have had lockdowns at school before after brown snakes were spotted on school grounds. Red-bellied black snakes are common around here too, and they're very dangerous, so I keep my head up and don't look down. I limp past the tennis courts and come around to the back of the group of kids, my chest tight and my breaths fast and heavy, in and out, and my leg shaking.

My eyes graze over everyone, looking for the usual group I run with. I spot Derek's white hair—he's in a group with Layla P. and Layla C. and Shamira, who aren't very fast at running. He waves to me, but my leg hurts so much and my fists are clenched so tight to help stop the pain that I don't wave back. He frowns at me, but I look away until I spot Jared and Rahul and Isaac. My insides become all twisty and a voice inside my head screams out at the burning in my thigh as I try to run over to them.

But my leg is too wobbly and I can't run anymore, so I stop and grab my thigh, and then I feel tears fall from my eyes and down my cheeks.

I grit my teeth and stand on a spot that doesn't have any grass, only dried-up dusty mud and small stones. My skin is hot and sweaty from the sun and from how fast I ran to get here in time. Inside my body I feel upset and angry, angry more than anything else—especially with Ms. Frisp for making me so late that I had to run and hurt my leg.

This is all her fault and it's not fair.

Jared comes over to me, Isaac and Rahul beside him. "What's wrong?" he asks.

I point to my thigh. "I hurt my leg when I was running here," I say, and then I see more people gather behind Jared, all peering at me and crowding around. I keep standing in the dirt, everyone else on the green grass, and I don't want to look at their faces and their eyes looking back at me, so I close my eyes, but when I do that their voices become louder and I can't stop myself from crying harder.

And my leg hurts so much, so I plonk to the ground on my butt.

A hand touches my shoulder and I don't shake it away because my brain is too full up with all the noises and the pain, and then I hear Mr. James clear his throat and say, "Okay, nothing to see here. Everyone apart from Alex's group, go off to the markers and wait for instructions."

I keep my eyes closed and feel the vibrations and hear the sounds of footsteps and murmuring children getting farther away. I find it easier to breathe but the pain is so bad and I can't stop crying.

"He hurt his leg," Jared says.

"Can you walk, son?" Mr. James asks, and I

frown, my eyes still closed, because of course I can walk. So I open my eyes and wipe the tears away with the back of my hand.

"Oh, that's a relief, I thought you were asleep for a moment there." Mr. James chuckles in his deep, scratchy voice.

I don't know why he says this because no one sleeps on the grass in PE. Mr. James always says strange things that don't make sense.

He chuckles again and then says, "Can I help you up?"

I nod, and he gently places one hand on the top of my arm and the other on my back. Jared comes to the other side of me and does the same, and I straighten my legs until I'm standing. I lock eyes on Mr. James's filthy white trainers and white ankle socks and hairy legs, which are thick like tree trunks—though they aren't that big, that's just what Mum said after we met him in the shopping mall once.

Jared lets go and right away the pain is so bad that I squeak and take all the weight off my right leg, and more tears start to fall.

"Is it your thigh?" Mr. James asks, and I nod. "Mmm, maybe a pulled muscle," he adds.

I've never had a pulled muscle before, I don't

think, because I don't remember having pain like this apart from the time I tripped over Kevin when we were playing chase in the hall and I banged my head on the wall as I fell.

"Okay, I don't think you can run today, my boy," Mr. James says.

I open my mouth to speak but I can't find any words and my tummy feels empty and I want to be sick.

"But what about our team?" Rahul asks.

"Yeah, we need four people for the relay, and we have to make districts," Jared says.

We've been practicing the relay race for three weeks, and each week my group comes in second and everyone high-fives me, and we might make it to districts. I don't really know what that is exactly, but Ned told me it's a big deal for fast runners. Our group always finishes behind Ella B.'s group in the relay, and Mr. James told us we'll definitely make districts if we run a tiny bit faster and cross the line under a certain time.

"Okay, okay," Mr. James says. "Well, there's only one other person who can run, and that's Ryan."

Jared and Rahul and Isaac all groan together and I groan too, though the pain in my leg stops it from coming out as loud as the others.

Ryan hasn't been allowed to run in PE for the past two weeks because he tripped Daisy on purpose and wouldn't try hard so his team came in last. Since then he's had to help Mr. James see who crosses the line first and put the cones out and collect them at the end of the lesson.

"Nope, no moaning. I will have a word with Ryan and make sure he runs fast, okay? I know how much districts means to you all. Now, off you go to your markers."

I watch Jared and Rahul and Isaac run off toward all the other kids spread out across the field on the soft grass, laughing and leaping and chatting and shouting, and I carry on standing in my dusty patch as more tears flood my eyes.

Everything is going wrong, but I have seen Ryan run and he's kind of fast, so maybe he can help get our team to districts.

"And that means, my boy, that I need someone to help me at the finish line." Mr. James is talking to me now.

I nod, my eyes still fixed on his trainers and socks and hairy legs, on his right toes tapping over and over.

"Will you help me out? Because these old eyes aren't what they used to be."

I glance up at Mr. James's face. He's older than Mum but I don't think as old as Ms. Frisp, and he has a bushy gray-and-black beard and eyebrows that match it, and he wears gold-rimmed glasses that are perfect circles. Now I wonder why he wears the glasses if he still can't see properly. I want to say this but I'm not sure if it's rude, and I've already been in trouble once today and I don't want that to happen again.

"Well, what do you think, Alex?"

I look down again, this time at the Jessops Lake badge on Mr. James's jersey, which is three white wiggly lines, one on top of the other, in the middle of a circle. It's meant to be the big lake in the center of town. I clasp my hands together, the sounds of cars driving past my school fading into the distance.

I think I can do the job, especially if it's important and Mr. James needs the help and I get to see who crosses the line first, so I nod. He shakes his fists in the air and says, "Awesome," and I smile because Mr. James is funny and nice.

"Come on, then, partner," he says. "Let's get to work."

CHAPTER THIRTEEN

"May I help you walk?" Mr. James holds out his hands toward me and I nod. He hooks his arm through mine and lifts me slightly as I start walking. The pain in my thigh is bad at first, but the more I walk and the more Mr. James helps, the easier it gets to keep moving.

Mr. James calls out more instructions to 6W and 6P, who wait on the running track in four groups, each next to a different colored cone: blue, yellow, green, and red. I always run the third leg of the race from the green cone, but today it will be Ryan. My tummy squeezes when I think about that and maybe I shouldn't have said I would help with an important job, but I also know I wouldn't be able to run fast today and this is our last chance to make districts.

We reach the finish line, where Ryan stands, his arms folded and his cap pulled low over his face so I can only just see his dark eyes.

"Ryan, my boy, you'll need to run today because poor old Alex here has hurt his leg."

I'm not old.

I peek at Ryan's face, waiting for him to say something rude, but he doesn't say anything or smile or frown or laugh. Ryan's face reminds me of the sad emoji and I wonder what might have made him sad, but then he shrugs and says, "But Mr. Leonard said I'm not allowed."

Mr. Leonard is the principal. My eyes widen because I didn't know Ryan had to go and see Mr. Leonard.

"I think it'll be okay, Ryan. Alex's group needs you. Isn't that right, Alex?"

I peer up at Mr. James, at his nice face that makes me think of Santa and his round eyes behind his round glasses, and he winks at me. Another wink. But Mr. James's wink doesn't make me angry because I think, like Ned said, that he's trying to make me laugh. He's always trying to make people laugh.

I don't want to laugh right now though.

"But I can't get in any more trouble, Mr. James, or Belinda won't take me to jujitsu anymore."

"Belinda?"

Ryan's eyes dart to mine and then back to Mr. James. "My foster mum."

I don't know what jujitsu is or what a foster

mum is, but Ryan looks even more sad now, or it could be a worried face. It makes me remember Derek's face last night when he spoke about fishing with his dad and how Ned and Mum's faces look sometimes now that Dad is away.

"But you're fast," I say, not sure if my voice is loud enough for anyone to hear.

"What's that?" Mr. James says, leaning one side of his head closer to my face.

I focus on the wiry curly hair of his beard. "Ryan runs fast and my group has to beat the time limit today and make districts." I want to add that if we don't make districts Jared won't want to be my friend and won't high-five me anymore, but I don't because the words kept getting quieter until they disappeared.

"Is that so?" Mr. James says.

I look at Ryan and see him frowning, his brown eyes staring right at me. I don't think I was rude to Ryan but his face isn't happy, and I'm not sure how he's feeling or if he's mad at me, so I look away.

"Okay, well, off you go, Ryan. You're running third leg, so do your best and get Alex's team to the districts, right?"

Ryan narrows his eyes at me a bit more and

I look away again quickly, my breathing fast. I press my back teeth together because I'm scared of Ryan even though he's not bigger than me, but then he nods once and runs off, his footsteps light and quiet on the grass.

Mr. James makes me sit on the other side of the finish line from him. The first runners are lined up a few steps away from us, their batons in hand, and I feel excited to see who crosses the line first. Mr. James raises his hand and shouts, "On your marks. Get set . . ." and my heart beats hard in a good way as he yells, "GO!"

Shouts and screams and cheers erupt from all the children, and even though it's loud I like the sounds and I clap my hands and shout too. Some of the kids are fast, racing out in front, but Isaac is the leader so far with a girl from 6P just behind him.

The batons are passed to the next children and off they go, racing to the green marker on the other side of the field where Ryan waits. I can't see who's winning from where I sit and my leg still hurts too much to stand up, so I carry on clapping and shouting because I want my team to win.

I see Ryan get the baton after two other people in different groups, but I can't tell who they are from over here, although I can see that they're way out in front. But then Ryan is running and he's being a good boy and not messing around.

And Ryan *is* fast!

He's catching up, and I scream louder and then he's rounding the corner. He hands the baton over to Jared and our team moves into second place.

Jared sprints, his arms pumping fast and his legs moving so quickly I wonder how it's even possible, and I wish mine would do that too. I stare at the finish line, waiting to see who crosses it first and hoping it's Jared.

The thudding, pounding footsteps rumble closer and closer and it makes me think of elephants. I stare at the line and then glance up at the runners, at how red their faces are. Jared and Ella are side by side and they cross the line together. Mr. James's stopwatch beeps and he scribbles numbers onto a small notepad with an even smaller pencil.

I let out a big breath and clap hard. I want to get up and cheer with Jared because he's never had a draw with Ella before, but then Mr. James tells me to get ready for the next groups, so I start looking at the finish line again.

Once all the final runners have crossed the line and Mr. James has made a note of everyone's times, he calls over the other runners, who crowd together.

Derek jogs over and sits down beside me. "Hi," he says, his cheeks bright red and his pale skin glistening in the sunshine.

"Hi," I say, and then I straighten out my legs, my thigh painful again and feeling tighter than before, like it won't work properly.

"Are you okay?" he asks, frowning down at my leg.

"No, I pulled a muscle, I think."

"Ouch."

I nod but then turn to face Mr. James as he calls for everyone's attention.

"Right, times are in, so let's see who's made the districts competition."

There's lots of whispering and I wish everyone would be quiet because it's harder to hear Mr. James, and I need to hear what he says because this could be my chance to make it to districts.

"Congratulations to Ella and Jared's teams, who finished under the time limit!"

Everyone cheers and Derek claps and I cover my ears and look for Jared and Rahul and Isaac. Our team made districts! I can't wait to tell Ned.

I remove one hand and clap it against my left leg and smile big until my cheeks hurt. I can't see the kids on my team, and my right leg hurts too much to move and find them, so I carry on sitting with Derek.

Mr. James tells everyone to grab a drink before we move on to long jump, and I realize I've forgotten my water bottle, but then Jared and Rahul and Isaac come over and I don't feel thirsty anymore. Ryan is walking with his hands in his pockets a short distance behind them as kids wander past and tell him how fast he ran. I smile at Jared, Rahul, and Isaac, but no one smiles back and I frown because I can't understand what their expressions mean.

Maybe they're coming to ask me to play with them at lunchtime now that our team made districts.

"Hey, Alex," Jared says, and then he looks over his shoulder and then back at me. "So, we made it to districts, but we think it's only fair that Ryan should be on our team if that's okay."

I stare at Jared, at the freckles on his nose and across his cheeks, and I listen to the words he just said in my mind again and again, and then I shake my head because it's not okay, but my brain isn't working and no words are coming, so I still don't say anything.

"Okay, sorry, Alex," Jared says, and then he runs off with Rahul and Isaac.

I see lots of other kids talking to Ryan now, and he smiles and shrugs as Jared's words sound in my head again, over and over, and all I can do is keep sitting on the ground until my shoulders and arms are too heavy to stay upright. I lie down and curl into a ball with my hands over my ears because I don't understand what to do with my body.

I hear Derek's voice beside me, and then other voices too, but nothing makes sense and so I just stare straight ahead until Mum comes.

CHAPTER FOURTEEN

Kevin licks my plate, *lick lick lick*, around the edges and down the middle, even though there's nothing left on it because I ate all the food and he's already licked it once. He even licks the fork until it falls off the edge and onto my blue blanket.

"Careful, Kevin," I say, putting the fork back on the plate with a clink.

Mum made me pasta with red sauce and cheese grated on top for dinner—my favorite—and she even let me eat it in bed and watch a movie on her iPad. I chose *Hotel for Dogs*. It's just finished and I've left the iPad on the blanket beside me because my leg hurts too much to reach over and put it on my bedside table. But Mum did tell me not to move and that she'll be back soon to collect my plate.

My chest feels heavy and my face numb, and my eyes are sore and swollen. I cried a lot after Mum brought me home straight after PE, or it might have been in the middle of PE. I can't remember because all my brain does remember is Jared telling me Ryan will be on the team for districts. Even thinking about it now brings new tears to my eyes, but before they have a chance to fall Kevin is licking my cheeks.

"Ew, stop," I tell him, gently pushing him back until I can see into his shiny big brown eyes. He sits and his ears tilt forward and he's making my favorite type of dog face, the one where I know he's waiting for me to speak to him.

I shudder in a breath, the type that only comes after I've cried a lot, and smile at him. "You can't lick me now because you've got pasta sauce all on your fur." I tickle his chin with my fingertips, avoiding the tufts at the front that are stained pink from the pasta. It's not a lot and he keeps licking his lips, so I think he'll have licked it all off before Mum comes in and sees.

Kevin leans forward a little, his head pressing down on my hand. He loves me tickling his chin, and after a minute he flops right down onto his tummy and across my left leg. He's sniffed my right one a lot since I got home but won't touch it.

I sigh and stroke Kevin's head, swirling his soft fur around my fingers and staring at his paws and nose and his eyes, which are still watching me.

"I don't think I will ever have a real friend," I

tell him. His ears prick forward slightly and I know he's listening. "I can't complete *Tunnels of Disaster and Doom* Map Five and now I can't be in districts because of Ryan." I take in another shuddering breath. "Maybe we shouldn't enter the contests at PAWS . . ."

Kevin's head lifts and he tilts it to one side, and I grind my back teeth together. We aren't going to win anything, I just know it, because that bald man with his Dalmatian will be there and he will definitely win everything, and there will probably be other dogs as brilliant as that Dalmatian, maybe even better. What's the point in going if I can't win a trophy?

There's a knock at my door and then Mum comes in, an Australian flag tea towel tossed over the shoulder of her yellow top. Her hair is tied back as usual and her face is a bit red and sweaty.

"Hey, baby," she says, then smiles with her lips closed, leaving my bedroom door open behind her. "How was that?" She points to my plate and I nod. "Good. I knew your favorite dinner would cheer you up."

My dinner was delicious but I'm not cheered up at all. I feel sad and tired inside and also on the outside, but I don't tell Mum because my head and my words are the most tired.

She sits on the edge of my bed on the other side of Kevin, and he shifts his head onto her lap. She leans over, lifting his head, and gives him a kiss on the top of it, then strokes his nose until his eyes start to close.

"I spoke to Dad earlier," she says, her eyes fixed on Kevin, with a smile that doesn't look like a happy one. "He misses everyone and can't wait to come home next month."

I don't like talking on the phone, but Mum speaks to Dad most days and tells me what he says. Dad says he doesn't mind and understands because he hates talking on the phone too. He'll come home soon anyway, so I'll talk to him then.

Mum continues, "I told him about the new family in number nine, about Wilma, and he said that was great. She's nice, isn't she?"

I nod because Wilma is nice and so are Derek and Mindy, and I wonder if Mum took over the cleaner that will get the stain out of the shower like she said yesterday, but I don't ask.

"They're renting the house for the next year." Mum smiles again, a little one, and shrugs, also a little one. "Looks like Ned and Mindy are getting along—he's over there now doing homework." She rolls her eyes. "And maybe Wilma and I can be friends too, who knows."

"How many friends did you have when you were at school?" I ask, patting Kevin's back.

"Hmm, when I was your age? I don't know, maybe two really good ones—let me think . . . Bella Stevens and Brad Finch. I had other friends, but those two were my best friends."

"But how many friends altogether?"

"I don't know, sweetie. It was a long time ago." She looks at me, blinking slowly. "You know, it's not important to have lots of friends, Alex. It's the quality that counts."

I frown, not sure what she means.

She sighs and adjusts her legs, crossing the right over the left. "I used to play with some kids, thinking they were my good friends, or I'd sometimes join a group because they were into something I liked, but do you know how I knew that Bella and Brad were my real friends?"

I shake my head, my hand stilling on Kevin's back.

"Because they were the ones who always saved me a seat in class or assembly, who shared their favorite things with me, who made me feel better if I was upset or if I hurt myself." She sighs again. "Darling, I know you want a friend more than anything in the world, but maybe you're trying too hard with the wrong kids."

"But . . . but I have to have a real friend, one of the popular ones, before secondary school or everyone will be mean to me," I say, clamping my back teeth together to hold back the fresh tears.

Mum laughs lightly. "Oh, that's not true. No one will be mean to you. Are people mean to you at school now?"

"Ryan is."

And Jared was today, but I don't want to say his name out loud.

"Yeah, well, you know what I think about Ryan? I think Ryan finds it hard to make friends too, and I don't think many people in Ryan's life say nice things to him, and that's why he says mean things to other people."

Mum narrows her eyes at me, and I think back to PE, to when I said Ryan was a fast runner and the face he made at me. I didn't know what his face meant or if he was going to be rude to me, and I wonder if he didn't understand that I was saying something nice. I feel sad for Ryan. I wish people would say nice things to him more often so he isn't mean to me all the time.

Mum lowers Kevin's head back onto my left leg and stands, then goes over to my window and lowers my blind. The darkening sky disappears behind the blue material, and the glow from my star lamp throws shadows across my room from my furniture and dog models and the giant cuddly toy basset hound that Nana and Grandad got me for Christmas when I was four that sits in the far corner.

Mum wanders back to my bed, leans over and kisses me on the forehead, and then picks up my plate. She pauses at the bedroom door.

"Alex, I'm old—well, not *old* old, but older than you—and I've had friends come and go from my life." She holds the door handle with her free hand. "And there have been times when I've been lonely and confused, when things have been hard."

"Like when Grandad died?"

"Yes, exactly, like when Grandad died. And those were the times when I realized there were some really good people who cared about me. I thought because I didn't see them all the time or speak to them on the phone every day, that meant they weren't my real friends. But they were. I just didn't see all the small wonderful things they did for me until I needed to."

I'm not sure what Mum means exactly or what small wonderful things are. I try to remember all of Mum's friends and the people who came round when Grandad died, but it was a long time ago and my memories aren't very good.

"Bad things don't last forever, and good always comes after bad, okay? You remember that."

I nod, but I'm not sure if she's right because I can't think of anything good happening after a bad thing.

"Anyway, sweetie, maybe try to get some sleep, okay?" Mum backs out of the room. "I'll let you off from brushing your teeth tonight so long as you promise to give me all the biggest smiles and rest that leg."

I nod and smile because I hate doing my teeth—two times every day!—and she smiles back with a small laugh before walking away. The soft padding of her bare feet disappears down the hall and then I hear her in the kitchen, doing all her usual cleaning-up jobs before she sits down and watches TV until bedtime.

I rest back against my squishy pillow, my head sinking down and my achy shoulders and neck feeling better straightaway. Kevin lets out a big yawn and climbs onto my pillow, wrapping his body around my head, his face on my right and his tail curled on the left. I rest my hand on his back and close my eyes, thinking about Ryan's face and Mum's words and wondering if Derek caught the bus home again after school.

THURSDAY, NOVEMBER 10

Two days to PAWS

CHAPTER FIFTEEN

I lie in bed on my left side, looking at Kevin, who's sitting by my bedroom door. His nose is pressed against it, low down near the floor, and it's like he's a toy, not moving, listening to all the sounds of the morning outside. I hear a scratch on the other side and then grumbling and a lazy woof that definitely came from Dennis. Kevin's tail wags from side to side, brushing the floorboards, and he sniffs at the door, but I don't get up to let him out because there's a lot of pain in my leg and I have a headache.

The handle turns and my door opens and Kevin scurries back, claws tapping against the wood. Dennis waddles in gurgling and grumbling, which is his way of saying hello. I know he's happy to see Kevin because his stumpy round tail is wiggling. He finishes saying good morning to Kevin and then flops past him and over to me, and he peeks over the side of the bed and licks his lips and gurgles a bit more.

"Morning, Dennis," I whisper, and then look up

to see Ned leaning against the doorframe. I catch sight of the back of Kevin as he whips past Ned and down the hall toward the kitchen, probably for his breakfast.

"All right, Alex," Ned says. "Can I come in?"

I nod and he enters, hands in the pockets of his school shorts. His hair is gelled over to the side again, and even though my room is still dark with the blinds rolled down, I can see his hair shimmer in the hallway light shining behind him. He also smells the same as he did the other morning, but I don't cough or say anything because Mum said we shouldn't.

He stands by my desk looking at my underwater puppy calendar and rubs one of his socked feet against his shin. "Not going in today, then?"

I shake my head and then croak, "No."

Mum came in earlier when she first woke up and before she had her shower, and I was already awake because my head was hurting and there was too much sadness inside for me to sleep. She said I could have the day at home and that she'd take the day off so we could do fun stuff together, though I don't really want to do fun stuff, even if it is the quiet fun stuff that Mum likes to do.

"Fair enough," he says, still facing my calendar. "Does your leg still hurt?"

"Yep," I answer, though at the moment, with it resting on top of my left leg, it feels okay.

"Bummer. I remember pulling a muscle in a football match once. Hurts for a bit but it'll go away." He turns and faces me, sitting back against my desk, and I hope he doesn't knock anything over because he's done that before, though this morning he seems quite calm and I don't mind him being in my room when he's like this.

"What're you gonna do today?" he asks, and I shrug because I haven't thought about it, though I am hungry, so I'll probably have some breakfast first. "Fair enough," Ned says again.

Dennis sits at Ned's feet and then collapses onto his belly. He licks the floor between his front legs with big long licks that are the opposite of Kevin's tiny quick ones. Ned runs a foot up and down over Dennis's back.

"Dennis will keep you company, won't you, you dork?" he says, but Dennis doesn't look up or even stop licking the floor, which is gross. I wonder what he can taste.

The *shush*ing of the running water in Mum's shower stops, and the sound of music from the kitchen trickles into my room along with the singing of birds outside and the smells of grass and trees and warm, fresh air, all through my open window.

"So, are you ready for the dog show on Saturday? Only two more days, right?"

I shake my head, not sure I want to talk about the dog show because for some reason that makes me think about what Jared said yesterday and the fact that I still haven't completed Map Five and that I still haven't got any real friends.

"Why not?" Ned asks, his forehead creasing as he moves the edge of my blinds aside with a fingertip and peers out, sunlight drenching his face.

"Because I won't win a trophy."

"Why won't you?"

"The bald man with the Dalmatian and all the other dogs like him."

Ned sighs and looks back at me, shoving his hand back in his pocket. "Nah, don't let that stop you from entering," he says. "So what if baldy goes? You should still enter just because Kevin is awesome and you'll have loads of fun."

I stare at Ned, at his dark eyes and brown skin and hair, and shake my head. "But I need the trophy," I croak, my throat dry and scratchy.

"No, you don't."

"I do," I say, forcing the words out a bit louder

because Ned's wrong. I do need the trophy but I won't win the trophy because Kevin isn't good enough to win.

Ned shakes his head. "Alex, trophies don't get you friends. They're nice to have and, like, you remember how you won them, but Mum just gets annoyed at all the dust they collect, and who wants that, right?" Ned smirks at me and I smile because Mum is always moaning about all the dust in the house and saying things like, "But I cleaned this just the other day."

There's a bang at the front door and Ned suddenly straightens and steps over Dennis.

"Ned," I hear Mum yell from her bedroom farther down the hall, and Ned rolls his eyes and shouts back "Yep," which startles me a little.

"Oops, sorry, Al," he says, and then comes over and ruffles my hair like he used to do before Dad went to work in the mines. "That'll be Mindy," he says, and his voice sounds quieter when he says Mindy's name, "because Wilma's giving me a lift to school today."

I nod and wonder what the inside of Wilma's Volkswagen is like and if it's blue like the outside.

"Have a good day, right? And make sure Dennis doesn't cause trouble." He smirks again and then plods out of my room, grabbing his schoolbag and shutting his bedroom door. He shouts bye to Mum, but then Mum rushes from her room and past my bedroom door in a waft of flowery smells.

Dennis never causes trouble so I don't know why Ned said that.

My leg and head hurt too much to sit up and peer out the window, but I listen to Mum and Wilma and Mindy's voices all saying "Hello" and "No problem" and "My pleasure" and "Thank you," and then I hear Derek's voice saying hi to Kevin and asking how I am.

I want to shout out and tell him about my leg and my head and how I'm probably not going to go to PAWS anymore and ask if he'll show me how to complete Map Five, but I don't because my brain is still too tired and heavy. Mum tells him I'm still sleeping and not to worry and to pop over later, and then I hear lots of footsteps scuff and clatter on the driveway as all of them leave. I follow the sounds across the road to the car at number nine, and then there are the thuds of closing doors and an engine starting up and a motor purring as they drive away.

And then it's quiet again except for the birds, and Kevin trots back into my room. He sniffs at Dennis, who's now sleeping in the spot where Ned stood, and then bounds up onto my bed and snuggles in next to me, smelling of his biscuits.

I don't stroke him because I'm too tired and comfortable under my blanket, but he doesn't seem to mind because sometimes we just like to be close to each other.

Mum's flip-flops slap as she comes up the hallway and enters my room, her hair wet and curly from the shower. She perches carefully on the edge of my bed.

"Just me and you today, sweetie," she says. I don't nod and I also don't correct her even though Dennis and Kevin are here as well. "Movie?" she asks.

"No," I whisper, and close my eyes.

"Okay, you have some sleep, then," she says, and I feel her hand rest on my forehead and then brush through my hair. "We can watch movies when you're ready."

I lie still, breathing in Kevin's dog smell and Mum's birthday shower gel smell and the lingering scent of Ned, and I listen to Dennis as he starts to snore. I know at some point Mum stands and tiptoes from my room but I don't care because I'm tired.

CHAPTER SIXTEEN

"Alex, you have a visitor." Mum peeks in my door and I sigh and hit pause on *OrbsWorld* to see who it is.

Kevin dashes in and leaps straight onto my bed without a sound, and as Mum steps aside, Derek appears round the corner, dressed in a plain white T-shirt and light green shorts. I think about all the clothes in my drawers and closet and I don't think I have any green clothes at all.

"Hey, Alex," Derek says, and then he pauses, one socked foot in my bedroom and one out in the hall. "Erm, is it okay if I come in?" he says, shifting his white hair out of his eyes with his fingertips.

"'Course it is, sweetheart," Mum says, placing her hand on Derek's shoulder. As Derek enters, Mum leans in and says, "Derek's mum and I will be having a cuppa in the kitchen if you need us," and then she skips off, reminding me of some of the girls at school.

"Hi," Derek says again, and I wonder why because he's already said hello once.

"Hi," I reply.

"Are you playing *OrbsWorld*?" he asks, and sits on the bed next to me, dragging himself backward until his back is leaning against the wall like mine. Kevin sprawls out in between us and faces the bedroom door. Derek stretches out his legs and crosses his ankles and I notice just how different the colors of our skin are.

Derek smells like a kitchen does when something yummy is cooking.

"Yeah, I just switched it on," I say, and look back at my laptop screen, hitting play and focusing again on choosing battle gear for my robot.

"*Tunnels of Disaster and Doom*?" he asks.

"Yeah," I say, and I want to ask Derek if he can help me finish Map Five, but inside my body I feel a bit scared and I don't know why, so I bite my back teeth together and click on my rock-climbing boots and golden winged helmet for my robot.

"Cool," he says.

I nod and enter the mud portal, which takes me underground to the tunnel entryways. The entries for Maps One to Four are surrounded by a yellow glow, which proves I've completed them, and entry six and the Trade Fair portal are boarded up with planks of wood, which tells me I can't go in yet.

In the middle is entry five and above it flashes READY? in big red letters.

I glance across at Derek but not at his face, though I can tell he's looking at the screen. I want to ask him for help, but I still don't, and I bite even harder with my back teeth.

"Are you feeling better?" Derek asks.

I nod. "Yep, my leg still hurts a bit but Mum's been giving me painkillers, so my headache is better and my leg doesn't hurt as much as it did this morning."

"Cool," Derek says again, and I think this might be his favorite word. "What did you do today?" he asks.

"Erm, slept mainly and, erm, watched movies with Mum."

Derek rests one hand flat on Kevin's butt, and Kevin moves his head up off the bed and then sideways onto Derek's shin. I hear a *tick tick tick* and glance down to see Derek flicking the nails of his thumb and pinky together over and over. "Kevin's a cool dog," he says. I nod and then Derek adds, "Jared was mean to you yesterday."

My insides tighten like I can't breathe and I quickly think about the breathing techniques I have to do when I'm feeling like this. I suck in and then blow out, in and out, because I do not want to start crying again.

"Ah, sorry, should I not have said that?" Derek asks, his fingers now digging into his skin. Kevin stands and turns around and then puts his head on my shoulder and licks my cheek.

"It's okay," I say, feeling a bit calmer, but I still don't want to talk about what Jared said or how much faster Ryan is at running than me, because today I wondered whether we would have made districts if I had run yesterday, and I don't want to think about that either.

"Okay," Derek says slowly, and I can see out of the corner of my eye that he's looking at me, until Kevin stops licking me and starts licking Derek's cheek instead. Derek giggles and tells Kevin to stop, which makes Kevin wag his tail and clamber on top of him and lick him some more.

Once Kevin is lying back down, Derek asks, "Which bit do you get stuck on in this map?"

"Where the ants come on the platform. I can never get out of the way in time and they always knock me off into the lava, and I have to get past them so I can get to the fair and Map Six and—"

I stop, glancing at Derek to see if there are any visual clues to tell me if he's still listening, and he looks right at me, so I think that means he is.

"Yeah, that bit's tricky, but I'll show you what to do when you get there."

My chest feels light and my heart beats fast, and I turn back to my laptop and hit enter. My robot spins and whizzes through the portal and then lands at the bottom of the ladder, ready to climb up and start Map Five.

"My mum brought over some cookies for you," Derek says as I hit the arrow keys and space bar to start maneuvering through the tunnel. "For Ned and your mum too. Do you like cookies? Mum made them herself just now; she's good at baking."

I nod. "Yeah, only soft ones though," I say, and then I wonder why I said that to Derek because when I told people at school once that I didn't like hard and crunchy foods, they laughed and said it was weird. But Derek says, "Yeah, these are soft ones, definitely," and that's it.

I carry on leaping and ducking my robot, and the platform with the ants is getting close. My heart is beating faster and I curl my toes.

"Okay," Derek says. "When you climb up the ladder to get on the platform, you have to hold down F for your flashlight and then you'll see a small box in the corner. You have to press the down arrow and hold it down to hide in there until the ants have all passed."

I nod as my robot climbs the ladder, and then I see it: a small brown box in the bottom right corner. I do exactly as Derek said. My finger presses the down arrow hard and my robot crouches down and slides into the box just as the ants scurry by, missing me completely.

"Now you can carry on," Derek says. "The rest will be easy for you because you're good."

I smile, my lips parting, and release the down arrow. My robot stands and I take him through the rest of the map, and Derek is right again: the rest of the map is easy. I tap the right arrow and hold S on the keyboard as fast as I can, my robot sprinting to the hole with END written above it, ants chasing me but not catching me.

"I DID IT!" I say, making Kevin stand and bark, his ears pinned back, and making Derek laugh and fall sideways on my bed.

"You're funny," Derek says, sitting back up, and I know he means it in a good way, not the rude way some people do, because his smile is big and shows off his white teeth and he's laughing now with his hand pressed to his chest. "You so made me jump."

I laugh too because I'm happy, definitely happy inside and outside. I finished *Tunnels of Disaster and Doom* Map Five and now I can go to the fair and complete the final map—Map Six! I watch the gold coins in the corner of the screen increase as my eighty million Orbsicles hit my pouch.

Once I've stopped laughing and Kevin has stopped licking our faces, I lean back against the pillow behind me and smile at my laptop. My robot is back at the tunnel entryways and there's a yellow glow around entry five and the boards are gone from entry six and the fair.

"Thanks for your help," I say to Derek, but I don't look at him in case he's looking at me.

"It's cool," he says, and I smile again.

I start on Map Six as Derek tells me about school today and *Skyscraper Escapades* and how Vinnie was sad when they left the house so he gave him a piece of cookie, and I tell Derek that next time he should bring Vinnie because that would make Kevin happy.

And then I hear Wilma call Derek's name, and Derek slides to the end of my bed and stands up. "Better go," he says, but before he leaves, he turns to look at me. "I like your room, by the way—you're really good at drawing."

I nod and look down at Kevin, my lips smooshed together because I don't know what to say. Mum always says that's okay because not many people know what to say to compliments.

"Oh, and Mum says we can go to the dog show on Saturday because Dad is going out of town for a conference. Are you still going?"

I look up at him standing by my door, his small pale hand gripping the handle, and then at Kevin, who is staring at me, his ears forward waiting for me to talk.

Yesterday was the worst day ever, but Mum was right when she said that good always comes after bad. If I could complete Map Five after not being able to for so long, then maybe there is a chance I can win that trophy and make a friend in time for secondary school.

I nod at Kevin and then at Derek. "Yep, Kevin and I will be there."

FRIDAY, NOVEMBER 11

One day to PAWS

CHAPTER SEVENTEEN

We all line up in twos outside the classroom door,
Ms. Westing at the front of all twenty-six of us
because no one is off school today—and that's
because today is the day of the special assembly.
Everyone knows it's going to be about PAWS, even
though none of the teachers or staff members have
actually said it is and it hasn't been written down
anywhere either.

I'm next to Angel because she asked if she could
walk with me in case my leg hurts too much and I
need help. I nodded when Ms. Westing asked me if
this was okay. I think Angel is the nicest person I
know, apart from Mum.

"Right, 6W, let's go!" Ms. Westing spins around
on her toes, her ankle-length cream dress, which
has brown paw prints all over it, swirling like she's
a dancer onstage. She's wearing her pumps again,
the same ones from Tuesday.

We all follow, me limping and only putting the
toe of my right foot on the ground. Angel is right by
my side. I don't look back because I don't want to

see Jared or Matilda or any of the other children's faces, so I glance at Angel instead, wondering if maybe she is an angel like Ms. Westing called her. But I don't think so, because Angel is an alive person and she doesn't have a halo.

There's no sun brightening the school grounds today as we make our way to the hall because the sky is filled with clouds, some white and some gray, and there's a wind blowing into my face that makes my cheeks sting a little and my nostrils feel even colder. Trees rustle all around me and I wonder if trees can feel cold too, and then I hear voices—lots of voices—as we get closer to the hall.

As the covered areas from all the classroom blocks merge into one wide walkway, I see kids from other classes arriving for the special assembly, and my breathing hitches and stutters at the sight of so many light blue uniforms.

I don't always have to attend assemblies because sometimes the noise and all the people give me too much anxiety, and my coping beaker fills up too quickly for me to control with breathing or tell anyone in time. I don't like it when other people are around me when I can't control my emotions because that's embarrassing.

But I have to attend this assembly to find out more about the dog show tomorrow.

So I clench my fists and my teeth and limp forward, my eyes flicking from Ms. Westing's dress to the hundreds of other kids around me to Angel's shiny black shoes walking in a steady rhythm.

There's laughter and chattering and squealing and shushing and teachers saying "Quiet down" and girls spinning and boys jumping and feet thumping. And I also hear music and children singing, and as 6W files in through the open double doors of the hall, I hear the words of the song, which is about a doggy in a window. I crane my head to see over and around all the other kids and teachers.

On the stage are two children I don't know singing into microphones. Behind them are other children dressed in costumes, which I think are supposed to be dogs, and they're dancing in front of some other Jessops Lake Primary School children who are playing violins. After the children sing a few words, everyone in the room claps twice, *clap clap*, and then this repeats.

We slow down as 6W shuffles into our seating area at the back of the hall, directly below one of the giant spinning fans on the ceiling, and Angel leads me to the end of the line, next to where Ms. Westing sits down on a chair at the outer edge of the hall by the window. I notice Ms. Frisp sitting in the chair behind Ms. Westing. She gives me a smile and a nod but she isn't clapping along with everyone else.

I remember that Ms. Frisp said she will give me back my notebook today and I wonder when, so I can show Angel.

It's loud—very loud—in the hall when everyone claps, *clap clap*, and I think all the children in all the classes are here in school today, even the sick ones. There are over a thousand kids in Jessops Lake Primary School and now they're all crammed into the school hall, and this thought sends a flutter through my chest.

Something inside the hall makes me feel happy today, even though my leg still hurts and I startle every time anyone claps. I shiver with excitement because I can't wait to see dogs on the stage.

I hope there will be dogs anyway.

The children finish singing and dancing, and then Mr. Leonard appears from behind the enormous maroon curtain that hangs on the right-hand side of the stage and strides forward. His brown suit is almost the same color as the stage and his jacket sleeves slide up his arms as he stretches them out to the sides.

"Welcome, children," he says without a microphone, because his voice is already loud and booming and reaches us all the way at the back of the hall. "First, we must give a big round of applause to Mr. Leitch's arts group for their song and dance routine."

The entire school erupts into cheers and applause, and I screw up my face and ram my hands over my ears as tight as they'll go. I feel Angel's hand on my shoulder but I don't take my hands off my ears until she taps me.

The hall has quieted again and everyone is sitting down. I follow Angel's lead and sit beside her on the shiny wooden floor, turning my head so I can see the open hall doors, which are only a few meters behind me, in case I need to leave. Ms. Westing says it's always fine if I need to step outside and get some fresh air.

But I hope I don't have to today.

Mr. Leonard is talking about the exciting event that is happening tomorrow and everyone in the whole room knows he's talking about PAWS. But when he announces it, actually says the word, everyone claps and cheers even louder than before. I cover my ears again but I keep looking forward this time as I watch the kids dressed as dogs and the singers and the violinists exit the stage, leaving Mr. Leonard in the middle alone.

"And today, we've organized a very special treat for you all," he continues once the room is quiet again other than a cough and some shuffling and the shifting of shoes and legs. "I would like you all to be as quiet as possible and remain on your bottoms so as not to startle today's guests."

There's a murmur of low and whispered voices rippling through the hall, and I pat my thighs gently, silently, waiting to see what will happen.

"Please welcome the PAWS Performance Pets." Mr. Leonard strides to the side of the stage, and from behind the maroon curtains appear six adults all dressed in bright yellow. They spread out, waiting and looking straight ahead at all the children, who are also waiting. Music that sounds a bit like the school orchestra starts to play, instruments like violins and flutes and other ones I don't know the names of, but no voices, and then the adults raise their right arms all at once.

Six dogs trot onto the stage at the same time,

each one going straight to what must be their owner. I clench my fists and shake my arms by my sides and smile at them. The first dog I see is a small poodle that looks a lot like Kevin—it could even be a cockapoo, it's so similar—and then there's a chocolate-brown Labrador, a Pekingese, a kelpie, a Jack Russell, and another brown dog I think must be a mixed breed.

As the trainers flick their arms and hands and dance side to side, crouching and moving back and forth, the dogs all obey the commands. They sit, stay, hop on one front leg and then the other, bow, lie down and play dead, and even stand with their front paws on their trainers' backs and point their snouts into the air.

I want to cry, not because I'm sad but because it's the best thing I have ever seen in my life. The dog I watch the most is the golden poodle like Kevin, and I start to wonder if maybe he can learn some of these tricks. And then the music stops and the dogs all sit by their owners and the owners say "Speak" all at the same time, and the dogs answer with two sharp barks.

Mr. Leonard wanders back onto the stage, but I don't listen to what he says because I'm staring at the dogs and replaying all the tricks I saw them do and wondering what it will be like tomorrow at the dog show and if there's still time to teach Kevin more.

The whole school is clapping again as the trainers and their dogs leave the stage, three to the left and three to the right, and this time I don't cover my ears because everything doesn't seem as loud as before.

I can only think about getting home to Kevin.

CHAPTER EIGHTEEN

Everyone is talking about PAWS.

EVERYONE.

It's lunchtime and I'm sitting in the tree garden by my classroom where it's quiet, but even here as I eat my ham sandwiches and banana, everyone I hear passing by, both children and adults, is talking about dogs. Recess was the same, and even in class after the assembly when we were supposed to be writing our short stories, all we did was talk about dogs. After lunch, in our final lesson of the week, Ms. Westing said we'll be allowed to share stories about our pet dogs, or stories about any dogs we might know. Or cats, because Ella B. prefers cats, she said, and everyone agreed that cat stories were okay too.

A flash of white hair passes the tree garden and I call out, "Derek!" before I can stop my mouth because he's the only person at school with hair that color. He stops and looks at me and waves, then strolls over to the bench where I'm sitting.

"Hi," he says. "Can I sit with you?"

I nod and so he does, placing his metal water bottle on the ground by his feet and taking the lid off his see-through lunchbox. He starts crunching on carrots from a small bag, dipping them in a pot of browny-yellow sauce that kind of looks like mustard but is much thicker.

He glances at me and I look away quickly, back at my own lunch, because Ned says it's rude to stare so I shouldn't do it, and I think sometimes I do but don't know it.

"It's called hummus," Derek says. "Want to try some?"

I stare at the dip and I don't think I do, so I shake my head. "No thanks," I answer.

"Cool."

We carry on eating, the wind still blowing and making the trees and leaves flap and shush around us. It's cooler today than yesterday but not cold enough that I need to put my sweater on. Mum says I'm quite a hot person and I think she's right.

"What tricks can Kevin do?" Derek asks, so I tell him all eight of the tricks we've practiced so far. "Cool," he says. "That's a lot of tricks. Vinnie can't do tricks," he adds, and then he laughs.

I'm not sure why he laughs but Derek's happy face is a lot better than his sad one.

"Do you like your dad?" I ask.

Derek has been swinging his legs back and forth but now they freeze for a moment. "Yeah, I like my dad," he answers eventually, his legs moving again.

"Why don't you go fishing with him anymore?"

"He's been too busy at work." Derek sighs and I wonder if I've said something I shouldn't have. "My mum and dad are getting divorced."

I've heard the word before but I don't know completely what it means.

"So yeah, Dad now lives in a different house from us, up in Brisbane."

I wrinkle my forehead, thinking about how Mum and Ned have been a bit sad since Dad went away to work, and I feel sad for Derek because his dad won't be coming back to his house but mine will.

We carry on eating and I think about the things that I know make Derek happy. "Will you enter Vinnie into a contest tomorrow?" I ask.

"Dunno," Derek answers with a shrug before biting into his kiwi fruit. He glances at me sideways but this time I don't look away. "Funny that my eyes are your favorite color and yours are mine, right?"

I nod. That is quite funny but I don't think I want to swap eyes because Mum says my eyes are like chocolate buttons and I like that they match Mum's and Ned's as well.

Someone stops by the entrance to the tree garden, blocking the light, and I look up to see Ryan standing there. I freeze, putting my half-eaten banana in my lunchbox and clipping the lid back on, *clip clip*, because once Ryan took my vanilla cupcake and took one bite before throwing it in the trash. I don't think Derek has noticed Ryan because he's still chewing his kiwi fruit and his legs are still kicking back and forth under the bench. I hope Ryan doesn't come any closer, but just in case he does, I take off my cap. I don't want him to whack it off like he usually does because sometimes that hurts and it messes up my hair.

But then Ryan raises one hand, and it looks like he might be waving at me. I frown back at him and wish I could see his face, but it's hidden beneath the peak of his cap and then he sprints off.

I keep frowning and glance sideways at Derek, who is still chewing and kicking his feet, and then I look back at where Ryan stood but all I see are kids in the distance dashing to and from the toilets.

I scratch my head and then put my cap back on, open my lunch, and finish my banana, watching a line of ants marching along the arm of the bench.

* * *

From my seat by the door, I can count the hands of eleven children stretching and waving in the air all trying to get Ms. Westing's attention. Everyone has a story they want to tell about their dogs—or cats—and we only have time for one more before the bell goes for the end of the day and the end of the week.

And that means PAWS is just one more sleep away.

"Okay, let's have . . . Matilda to finish."

"Yes!" Matilda shouts, and shoves her chair back with a loud scrape that makes me narrow my eyes a bit and shudder, but even though I still don't like Matilda because of what she did on Tuesday, I am interested in her story, so I keep looking ahead like all the other kids.

I haven't put my hand up even though I think 6W would like the story about Kevin running away to

Derek's house and making dog friends with Vinnie. Standing at the front of the class means everyone will look at me.

My favorite dog story so far is Joshua's, who told us about the time his family went to the rescue center to get one small dog but came home with three big ones. He said he, his mum, and his dad each chose the one they liked best and they couldn't decide, so they got them all. He also said it was a sad place and his mum cried and that they wanted to bring more dogs home. I don't think I want to go to the rescue center because even hearing Joshua's story about the dogs in the small cages made me want to cry.

Ella B. was picked to talk about her cats—two tabbies and one Siamese—and Wu and Isaac and three more children told stories about their dogs or dogs that belong to their neighbors or their family members.

It seems that everyone loves dogs—or cats. This afternoon has been the best ever and all the kids in 6W have been happy and friendly and nice to each other and to me, asking how my leg is and if I'm going to PAWS tomorrow, and I think this is all because of how dogs make people happy.

I haven't spoken to Jared yet. He's sitting next

to Ella and looking down at his desk and his expression looks sad. I wonder what's wrong with him but then Matilda starts to tell her story and her voice is loud, which makes Jared look up.

"My nana and papa's dog is a diabetes dog and has saved my papa's life," she says, her words slow and slurred but still clear enough for me to understand.

"Wow," says Ms. Westing. "That really is amazing. What's your nana and papa's dog's name?"

"Alex," Matilda answers, and all the heads in 6W turn to face me at the same time. My heart pounds, *duh duh duh*, and I swallow and look down at the wooden tabletop, at my rainbow of pencils and my green robot notebook that Ms. Frisp gave to Ms. Westing at lunchtime to return to me.

"Well, how about that?" Ms. Westing says, and I wonder what she's going to say next. "Obviously Alex is a name given only to very special friends."

Angel nudges me, and I hear the murmurs of other children in the class as they talk to each other. I wish I could hear the words they're saying but my heart is beating too loud in my ears and I just keep looking at my pencils. I realize I'm smooshing my lips together because what Ms. Westing said was a compliment.

But I don't know if it's true because none of the children in my class are my real friends.

"Thank you, Matilda," Ms. Westing says, and then the bell sounds. "Before you go," Ms. Westing continues in a big outdoor voice, "I would like to thank you all for being so well behaved today and for sharing your dog stories—"

"And cat stories!" Ella shouts, and all the other kids and I laugh.

"And cat stories," Ms. Westing repeats. "I know there are a lot more of you who have stories but didn't get to tell them, but that's okay, because I think we all agree that dogs—and cats—make wonderful friends and perhaps we should all try to be more like them."

I hear giggles from some of the children and others make barking sounds, but I am sure Ms. Westing doesn't mean we should do that or to walk around on all fours and eat from bowls on the floor without knives and forks. This makes me smile.

"I hope to see you all tomorrow at PAWS! Good luck to those entering their dogs into the contests."

And then the classroom erupts into the sounds of children packing away their things, pushing their chairs under their desks, and rushing from the room.

I focus on putting my pencils away and then Angel taps the desk in front of me before resting her palm on the robot notebook.

"May I take a quick look now?" she asks.

I glance across at her, at her black hair and pale skin and kind eyes, and I nod.

She flicks through the pages and I continue packing away my things. I stand and slide my chair under my table, and Angel closes my book.

"Wow." She smiles at me. "Just wow, Alex. You should start sharing your sketches with more people."

I smile, trying not to smoosh my lips.

"Come on, Angel." We both turn and see Linda holding open the classroom door, her schoolbag already over her shoulder.

"Coming," Angel says. She turns back to me and hands me my robot notebook. "I'm sleeping over at Linda's house tonight. Thanks for showing me these sketches. See you tomorrow at PAWS." Quietly, her shoes *pad pad pad* from the classroom.

I hug my notebook to my chest and wonder what sleepovers are like.

SATURDAY, NOVEMBER 12

Zero days to PAWS

CHAPTER NINETEEN

I throw Kevin's ball for him, a small throw, underhand, straight toward his mouth, and this time he catches it perfectly. "Yes!" I say, shaking my clenched fists in triumph. Kevin trots over and lets me take Ned's pink ball from his mouth. Ned saw me playing with it after school yesterday but didn't ask for it back, so I wonder if he's forgotten that it's the one I took from his room.

It's ten minutes to nine. Kevin and I have been up since five, but Mum wouldn't let us come outside to practice last-minute training until seven thirty, so we trained in the hall until then. Because I couldn't throw the ball far inside, I did small throws, and that's when Kevin started to catch the ball every single time.

"Good boy," I say to Kevin, rubbing my cheek against his face. In return he licks me on the tip of my nose, which makes me laugh. "Shall we make the throw a bit bigger this time?" His ears rock forward and then he backs up a bit, tail wagging, his front legs bent and ready. I throw the ball and he catches it again and then brings it straight back to me. "You did it!" I tell him, and this time I wrap my arms around his small soft body and hug him. He rests his chin on my shoulder and licks my ear, the *lap lap* sound of his tongue as tickly as the wet feel of it.

"I hope Mum and Ned come out soon so we can leave." It isn't far to Jessops Lake Showground, maybe a five-minute journey in the Mitsubishi Outlander, but Mum said "parking will be a nightmare" and I think she means there will be a lot of cars. "Registrations open at eight a.m.— that's what the poster and the website and all the flyers say—and we can't be late." I grind my back teeth together and then Kevin licks me faster, pulling away from my hug to get my face. "You're so silly," I tell him.

I hear a click and voices and then the *yap yap* of a small dog, and I look over at 9 Cantering Court to see Vinnie charging across the road. Kevin bounds over to him and they meet in the middle of the road and start growling and jumping up, paws batting each other.

"Vinnie!" Derek calls, jogging down his drive and over to the dogs, who have made a circle with their bodies just like before, sniffing each other's bottoms. I don't step off the grass edge of my yard because Mum says I can't ever go onto the road without her, no matter what.

"Hey, Alex," Derek says as he bends over and clips a black lead onto Vinnie's red collar. He walks over and Vinnie and Kevin follow, still sniffing and pawing each other.

"Hey, Derek," I answer. "Are you going to PAWS?" I see Mindy and Wilma coming out of the black door of number nine, and Mindy waves and Wilma says hello before they climb into the blue Volkswagen in the driveway.

"Yep. Mum thinks parking will be a nightmare," Derek says.

"My mum said exactly the same thing."

"Are you leaving soon too?"

I turn back to my house but neither Ned nor Mum comes out the screen door. "I think so."

I hope so.

"Cool," Derek answers. "Well, see you there, then. Bye, Kevin." He leans over and pats Kevin's head, and Vinnie gives Kevin a quick *yap yap* as they walk away and climb into the back of their car. The engine grumbles as Wilma starts it up, and I crouch beside Kevin, my fingers hooked into his collar so he doesn't run in front of the car. I wait until it rolls off the driveway and disappears slowly around the corner.

When I can no longer hear the engine, I straighten and head back inside, tucking the pink ball in the pocket of my blue shorts. As the screen door bangs shut behind me, I hear Mum knocking on Ned's door.

"Ned, we have to go now," she says, her words coming out slow and a bit angry. I edge to the corner and peer round to see her standing with her hands on her hips outside Ned's room. "Ned!" she bellows, and I startle. Kevin sits at my feet, his back pressed against my shins.

"I'm coming!" I hear Ned yell back from behind his closed door.

"You'd better, because you know how much today means to your brother." Mum turns then and when she sees me she spreads her arms and smiles, lots of her white teeth showing. "Hello, my superstar son," she says, clasping her hands in front of her long-sleeved blue shirt. "Are you ready to go? Teeth, socks, shoes?"

"Is Ned ready? We have to go now because Derek and Mindy and Wilma have already left." My cheeks feel hot even though it's not a hot day and I think it's because inside I'm nervous and excited and scared that we're going to be late.

"Don't you worry about Ned. I'll have him ready." She gently places both her hands on my shoulders and I don't mind or wiggle them off. "Now, you go finish getting ready and I'll grab some water bottles, got it?"

I nod and do as she says, Kevin beside me the whole time—sitting by the bathroom door while I brush my teeth, waiting by my bedroom door as I find my favorite blue socks in my bottom drawer, and standing beside me as I cram my feet into my trainers, the laces already done up so I don't have to do them.

Mum hands me a small backpack. "Pop this on your back today. Inside are two bottles of water for you and one for Kevin, along with his water bowl. You're going to need it." She grins and winks, and this time I like the wink, so I smile back.

"Right, go hop in the car—it's already open. I'll get Ned." She says the last words through gritted teeth and then strides down the hall to his door, her flip-flops making more of a booming sound on the wooden floor than the usual *slap slap*.

As she thumps on his door, which I know she

does with the side of her fist because I've heard that sound before, and shouts his name, I grab Kevin's lead from the hook, fill up my pockets with dog treats, and hop out the screen door to the car. I open the back door and Kevin leaps inside and immediately lies down and starts licking his privates. I sit next to him on the soft seat and my heart judders and my hands shake. Right now I can hardly feel the strain in my right thigh because finally we're on our way to PAWS.

CHAPTER TWENTY

The digital clock on the black dashboard flicks to 9:43 just as Mum shuts down the engine. The stench of Ned's deodorant or whatever it is he's wearing burns the inside of my nostrils, and I shove open the door, sticking my head out and sucking in as much fresh air as I can. Music vibrates and rumbles close by, accompanied by shouts and laughter, barking and yapping, and the smell of smoke and barbecued food.

I take deep breaths through my nose and release them through my mouth, but not because I'm angry or sad or anything like that. I'm so excited my head and chest feel like they might burst. I only ever feel like this at Christmas and on my birthday.

Ned's door opens and he steps out, his trainers looking even whiter on the bright green grass than I've ever seen before. He straightens and looks at me as I shut the car door behind me and grip Kevin's blue lead with my other hand.

"All right, Al," he says, smoothing a palm over his already sleek hair. "You and Kevin ready for this?"

I nod, even though I'm not completely sure we are. Right now I can't stop looking at Ned and his gelled hair and his smart red shirt and jeans. He looks different today—like Ned, but not like Ned.

"What?" he asks, his neck and cheeks turning a bit red, like his shirt. "What?" he asks again, this time making two little lines between his eyebrows as he frowns at me and pats down his hair at the back.

"I think you look really cool," I say, which makes me think of Derek and how that's his favorite word. I do think Ned looks awesome today, more awesome than he's ever looked.

Ned's face changes, his frown disappearing and his eyes crinkling at the edges as he smiles. "Cheers, bro," he says, and shoves his hands in his pockets.

"Right, you two," Mum says. "We need to get over to Registrations pretty soon."

"Come on, Kevin," I say, my tummy dipping and rising and my hands trembling a little bit, and we set off behind Mum, weaving between the cars. There are hundreds of them, all parked in rows as far as I can see in every direction.

I hope we can find our car later when we have to leave.

It took us ten minutes of sitting in traffic to make it to the car park entrance, where adults in bright green vests waved at us to turn right, and then we drove for more minutes following more adults in bright green vests waving us on until eventually one last adult pointed to where we should park the car. Mum turned off the radio so she could concentrate, and Ned and Kevin and I stayed quiet because sometimes Mum says rude words in the car when she has to concentrate.

And now I can see that Jessops Lake Showground doesn't look like Jessops Lake Showground today.

There's a long row of huge tents set up at the bottom of the car park, maybe more than ten—I can't count because there's so much noise and activity and my brain can't focus on one thing—and people and dogs are *everywhere*. Children and adults and puppies and dogs of all shapes and sizes, including breeds I've never even seen or read about, are all heading toward the tents or standing inside and waiting in groups and lines.

I'm sure my heart has never beat this hard before, and I think Kevin is just as excited because he keeps sniffing at other dogs as they pass, gently tugging my arm this way and that, but also looking up at me as if to make sure I'm still there.

I'll never leave Kevin.

"You okay with all the noise and people?" Mum asks as we near one of the beige tents with a sign saying REGISTRATIONS in big black letters hanging over the entrance, the Chinese crested dog picture on each end of the sign. The music and voices are louder here, and there are lots of people crowded into this tent, all talking, their dogs on leashes sniffing other dogs, cocking their legs and squatting, sitting and scratching their ears, jumping up on their owners . . .

My eyes can't take it all in at once. My emotions are whirling inside me, making me feel like I might cry or laugh or shout out loud, but I keep them bottled up, squeezing Kevin's lead as hard as I can until my fingers and wrist hurt, my other hand clinging to the backpack strap over my shoulder.

I feel Mum's hand enclose mine and Ned's hand on my shoulder.

"Alex? All good?" Mum asks.

I nod. I don't know if the noise and people will be okay, but I know this is where Kevin and I need to be.

Ned scoops up Kevin, who I realize is standing with his paws on my thighs, and kisses him on the nose before handing him to me. I take Kevin, inhaling deeply as I hug him close to my chest. His soft fur makes me feel calmer, but he's not licking me at the moment, just resting his head on my shoulder, his ear like velvet against my cheek.

"Okay," Mum says. "So, I think we have to join this line and speak to the lady sitting at the desk over there."

There are adults in red T-shirts standing at the edge of the tent. One lady with darker skin than mine and long dark hair about the same color as mine holds a clipboard and is looking right at me. I quickly move my eyes away and then, through a gap between all the people, notice the lady Mum must be talking about. She's older than Mum and has glasses and gray hair and she's wearing a red T-shirt too. She's holding a pen and writing things down on a piece of paper and handing other different-colored bits of paper to each person as they reach her table. And then the people take their pieces of paper and move to the back of the tent, where they are ushered through small doors and walkways and into the main part of the showground—into PAWS.

I'm scared my heart will beat so fast it will get tired too quickly, because now I can feel it drumming in my neck and against Kevin's body.

But Kevin doesn't move, still as a statue in my arms, and I keep hugging him gently, scritching and scratching his back with my fingernails, my other hand under his bottom, holding him up.

And then we're next, standing in front of the gray haired lady, who's sitting at a white table covered in neat piles of paper.

"Hey there!" she says. "Welcome to PAWS Dog Show! Are you entering your pooch into a contest today?"

I nod.

"And what contest would you like to enter?"

I stare at her, my brain trying to remember the right words, the words I practiced last night as I brushed Kevin with my special glove brush.

The lady stares back, a friendly smile on her face, her pen poised above a piece of paper that has a grid on it with four columns and lots and lots of writing.

"Alex?" Ned says in a low voice. "Do you want me to tell her?"

I shake my head because my brain has found the words, though my voice only comes out as a whisper. "Obedience."

"Okay . . ." She looks down at her papers, flipping

through until she finds one with OBEDIENCE printed across the top. "Oh, honey, that contest is full up."

Seriously? Full up?

She looks back up at me. "Do you have another choice?"

I frown and say, "Tricks," but still in a whisper.

"Okay . . ." she says again, and finds the piece with TRICKS on the top. And then she shakes her head and I'm starting to feel strange and Kevin is feeling heavier in my arms.

"I'm afraid that's full up too," she says. "You've chosen two of the most popular contests."

Mum puts her arm around me, and I concentrate on the softness of her shirt against my neck. Kevin adjusts his head and puts his snout under my chin, pressing it up gently.

I hear the lady say, "If you'd come earlier, then you might have made it in time," but I don't look at her or respond because I know she's right.

Everything Kevin and I have been practicing— the sitting and the staying and the spinning and even catching his ball this morning—has all been a waste of time.

And now I will never get a trophy.

CHAPTER TWENTY-ONE

"Do you have any other choices, honey?" the lady asks.

"What do you think, Alex?" Mum asks, and I don't think anything because my brain has stopped, completely stopped. All the noises from before, the voices and the laughing and the barking and yapping and whining and cheering . . . they've all become a low buzz in my ears and everyone around me seems to have faded into the background and my feet don't feel like they're standing on the ground. The only things I can focus on are the feel of Kevin's soft fur and the gentle movement of his chest and sides as he breathes in and out.

Everything is ruined.

All because Ned made us late.

"Can you tell us what contests aren't full up?" Mum asks, and the lady says, "Sure," and then I hear the flicking of paper as she searches through her pile.

"Okay, we have . . . Smallest and Biggest, so no, neither of those seem right . . ." More flicking of paper. "We have Best Outfit . . . nope. We have Fluffiest and—oh, here's a good one. We have Happiest."

I glance at the lady, letting my eyes focus on her wrinkly face again. She looks back at me with that same friendly smile, and I notice a splodge of pink lipstick on her front teeth.

"He does look like one happy dog," she says, her eyes traveling down to Kevin and then back up to me. "What do you think?"

I draw my head back and Kevin does the same, and I stare into his brown eyes as he stares into mine.

"Kevin's definitely a happy dog," Ned says on my right.

"I second that," Mum adds on my left.

"What do you think, Kevin?" I ask, still whispering, and he gives me two long licks across my nose. I nod at him and then at Mum. "Okay, we'll enter that one."

"Awe-some," the old lady says, drawing out the word in a singsong voice.

She writes something on the piece of paper and then hands me two rectangles of purple cardboard with the number thirty written on them in thick black ink.

"These are your entrant numbers, so don't lose them. Your contest takes place in arena four at eleven thirty, so get there ten minutes early. Okay?"

I nod and take the numbers, not sure if I'll remember everything she just said, and Mum thanks her and pushes me gently toward one of the doorways at the back of the tent. I cling to Kevin as we step from the clear plastic under our feet back onto soft grass, and then I see it.

The PAWS Dog Show.

I have never seen Jessops Lake Showground as busy as it is now, and there is so much to see in every direction. We step forward slowly and I place Kevin on the ground, gripping his leash as tight as I can. Dogs and their human families walk this way and that, crossing paths, and I wonder how everyone isn't crashing into each other.

Voices come from speakers sitting atop posts, announcing the day's schedule and the contest times and where we can buy food and drink and where to meet Australia's biggest dog and rainbow poodles and police dogs and where to sign up to adopt a dog . . .

And my ears and brain can't keep up.

I take some deep breaths and follow Mum as she weaves through the passing people and pets until we come to a post with seven handwritten signs: FOOD, TOILETS, and STALLS point to the right, and DISPLAYS, ATTRACTIONS, and ARENAS to the left. The other sign, EXIT, points back the way we just came. Mum turns and leans down to speak in my ear.

"Where do you want to go first?"

I look into her eyes and grind my back teeth together, thinking about what I'd like to see, but I don't know because there's so much to remember and my brain still isn't working quickly enough.

Mum tucks her hair behind one ear and raises her eyebrows, and then she nudges Ned, who's texting on his phone beside me. "Really?" she asks him.

"It's okay, I'm finding out something," he says with a sideways smirk like the ones Derek does.

Mum shakes her head. "Whatever, just please don't be on that thing all day, okay?"

Ned nods, his eyes still on his phone, and then he switches it off and puts it in his pocket. He narrows his eyes at me and asks, "Why don't we head over to the giant dog display? They've got Saint Bernards and Irish wolfhounds, apparently."

I wonder how he knows that but nod and give Kevin's leash a slight tug. "Come on, boy," I say to him. "Let's go see your giant brothers." His ears go back and he wags his tail and we set off again, heading left toward Attractions.

We pass the rainbow poodles, where big versions of Kevin sit on platforms, but they all have longer and much curlier fur, which is cut in strange shapes and colored so they look like rainbows. I'm not sure I like that people do this to their dogs. I glance down at Kevin, who has his mouth closed and his ears forward, which I think means he's not very happy about it either.

"Don't worry, I won't do that to your fur," I tell Kevin, but I don't think he hears me.

Next is a marquee with a POLICE DOGS sign over the top. Inside are beautiful German shepherds with black-and-brown fur and ears that point up. Some are lying down sleeping while others chew bones and others sit perfectly still at the feet of police officers.

"Looks like they're chilling out before their display," Mum says, and I think she's right, because that doesn't start until later this afternoon.

A bit farther on is another tent. Inside are some Labradors and golden retrievers, and I don't need to see the sign to know they're guide dogs. Each wears a blue jacket and has a special harness held by an adult or child who wears a matching blue jacket. I love guide dogs and think they do the most amazing job.

And then I remember Alex, the diabetes dog that belongs to Matilda's grandparents. I don't know what diabetes is, and I wonder if I could ask Matilda some questions one day.

"Alex!"

I look away from the guide dogs and see Derek waving and Mindy and Wilma standing on either side of him. They're all beside a sign that says GIANT DOGS. A *yap yap yap* makes me look down and then Kevin pulls on his leash and I know it's because he wants to go see Vinnie, so I run with him until the two dogs are leaping and circling each other.

"Hey," Derek says, and I say hey back.

"Well, hello there, Alex and his wonderful family," Wilma says, and she and Mum hug and kiss each other's cheeks and I wonder if maybe they're friends now.

"Hi, Alex," Mindy says in her gentle voice, and then she stands beside Ned, who flicks his hair. I notice his cheeks are a bit red again.

"I'm pleased you could come and find us, Alex. Derek has been looking for you since we arrived," Wilma says, her arm linked with Mum's. "You must go and see the big doggies in this tent. They are ginormous."

"They are massive," Derek says, and spreads his arms wide.

I look at Mum and she nods, so Derek and I lead the way into the GIANT DOGS tent.

Wilma and Ned are right. There are Saint Bernards and Irish wolfhounds and other dogs like mastiffs and Great Danes. Vinnie yanks Derek this way and that as he tries to greet every dog with a yap and a lick, and I laugh at Derek as he stumbles and trips and tries to pull Vinnie back. Kevin walks like a good boy and stands in front of me the whole time we're looking at the dogs, and I wonder if he's protecting me in case they attack. I pat his head often and tell him how good he's being and he wags his tail each time.

We wander out of the GIANT DOGS tent with Vinnie out in front, then Kevin just in front of Derek and me. Wilma and Mum are behind us, and Mindy and Ned at the back. Apart from Mindy being a girl, our families are exactly the same, and I smile because I like that.

"Did you enter Kevin in the Obedience contest?" Derek asks.

I screw up my face and shake my head. "No, we were too late."

"Oh. What about the Tricks one?"

"No, we were too late for that one too."

"So are you entering any contests at all?" Derek asks.

"The only contest left that Kevin could enter was the Happiest contest, so we entered that one."

"No way!" Derek says, putting one hand on his head, though I don't know why. "I entered Vinnie in that one too! We can go together!"

I smile and nod lots of times, because knowing Derek and Vinnie will be in the contest with me makes me feel less worried and even more excited.

"This is so cool," Derek says as we look around.

"Yeah, it's cool," I say, and Derek laughs and I smile even bigger because I like Derek's laugh.

After some more time wandering through the attractions, we come to an archway with ARENAS written above it, and my stomach twirls and spins.

"Can we go watch some of the contests?" Derek asks his mum.

"Is that okay with you, Kim?" Wilma asks Mum. Mum looks at me, chewing on her thumbnail.

"I don't know," she says, and I know it's because

she worries about me, especially somewhere like this with so many people and so much noise.

"It's okay," Mindy says. "Ned and I can stay with them if you two want to go and have a coffee."

Wilma and Mindy touch foreheads, looking into each other's blue eyes, and then Wilma kisses Mindy on the forehead and strokes her long white hair and tells her she's a "perfect princess." I see Mum's fingers dancing by her sides like she has pianos on her thighs, and I remember from the Be Aware classes that this sometimes means someone is nervous.

"I'll be fine, Mum," I say.

"Yeah, I won't leave him," Ned says, placing a hand on my shoulder.

Kevin barks up at Mum and Mum laughs. "Okay, you go, but stick together, got it?"

"Yep," I say.

Wilma hooks her arm through Mum's again and pulls her away, and they both wave. "We'll come and find you right here at the entrance to the arenas in one hour for the Happiest contest," Wilma calls back over her shoulder.

"Right," Derek says, his right arm stretched out as Vinnie yaps and tries to run under the archway and into the arenas. "I think Vinnie knows where to go."

I glance back at Mum as the six of us, four kids and two dogs, move forward. As the back of her blue shirt is swallowed up by the crowds, I notice the woman with the clipboard who was looking at me earlier now standing a short distance away— and she's watching me again.

I quickly turn away with Kevin by my side, wondering what she's writing on that clipboard.

CHAPTER TWENTY-TWO

We find some empty green seats at arena two and we all sit in a line, me sandwiched between Derek and Ned, Mindy on Ned's other side. Kevin sits at my feet and yawns. The seats are hard and uncomfortable and a bit slippery, but I don't mind because it means I can rest my leg, even though it feels better today. In two minutes it's the start of the Obedience contest, and I want to watch and see how good the dogs are.

I wonder if the bald man is here with his Dalmatian.

Arena two is a big grassy square area with a thick black line all the way around the outside. We had to climb some stairs to reach the seating area on one side. There are tables covered in black tablecloths all around the outside of the square and adults in smart white shirts sitting at them. I wonder if they're the judges. My tummy somersaults as I think about how soon it will be Kevin and me being judged, but then it relaxes when I remember that Derek and Vinnie will be there too.

Derek's purple rectangle has number twenty-two on it, but I hope we'll be able to be near each other.

I remove my backpack and take out a water bottle and Kevin's bowl and pour him a few glugs. Kevin and Vinnie immediately start drinking, *lap lap lap*, splashes of cold water dotting my shins, and I like that Kevin is sharing his water with Vinnie. Kevin has a friend, a dog friend, and I wonder if that makes him happy.

A man's voice booms through the speaker, announcing that the contest is about to begin, and then music pumps out and the crowd starts cheering and clapping as dogs and their owners file into the arena. Ned looks at me and I nod. I think he's worried about me and the noise, but I'm not scared.

I think there are about thirty dogs. As they walk, each owner holds up a yellow rectangle with a number on it, like my purple one, which they show to the judges, and then they each find a space inside the grassy square in the middle.

And then it begins.

They have ten minutes to show the judges exactly how obedient their dogs are. As the massive clock on the screen in the corner counts down, Ned and Mindy talk quietly on my right, laughing and smiling, and Derek points and says "Wow, look at that dog" more than once on my left.

As owners stride back and forth and turn their backs on their pets and call out instructions, the dogs lie down, sit, and come the second each command is given. Then they walk perfectly pressed against their owners' legs, looking up at them expectantly.

I swish my lips left and right and look down at Kevin, who's sleeping at my feet, and I feel glad that we didn't enter the Obedience contest. Although Kevin can do most of those things, he isn't as quick, and sometimes I have to give a command more than once.

With only ten seconds to go, the owners finish up with one last command, and then a buzzer sounds to signal the end of the contest and all the dogs get put back on their leashes.

"Wow!" Derek says as the dogs trot out of the arena, the owners once again flashing their yellow cards at the judges. "There were some seriously cool dogs out there."

At the same moment, Derek and I look down at Vinnie, but he's not there. Derek holds the end of his leash, which trails down beneath his seat, so we both lean forward and look under. Vinnie is lying down and chewing loudly, making a *smack smack smack* with his mouth, and between his paws is a brown paper bag with HENRY'S H written across it in red letters. I think it should say HENRY'S HOT DOGS, but Vinnie has already eaten the OT DOGS part.

"Oh Vinnie," Derek says, taking the paper bag and crumpling it up. "You're so disgusting."

Vinnie crawls out and immediately starts pawing at Kevin, and Kevin rolls onto his back, kicking his legs out at Vinnie.

I giggle and look at Derek's screwed-up face. "Vinnie's so funny," I say to him, and he nods.

"You want to stay here and watch?" Ned asks me, pointing at the screen above the arena. I follow his finger and read NEXT UP: TRICKS!

"Yep," I answer. I turn to Derek. "Want to watch the Tricks contest next?"

"Ooh, defo. Cool," Derek says, and so we stay where we are on the uncomfortable green seats as other spectators leave and new ones arrive around us, rustling food packets and chatting about the dog show. Kevin goes back to sleep, his head on my feet, as Vinnie heads back under the seats, probably looking for more wrappers to eat, and Ned and

Mindy talk and look at their phones. Derek starts telling me about *Skyscraper Escapades* on *OrbsWorld* and how in each level you have to make it to the top of a skyscraper before an earthquake makes it fall down. It sounds awesome.

We keep talking about *OrbsWorld* as the man's voice returns over the speaker to announce the start of the Tricks contest, me asking Derek questions and him answering them, until the dogs and owners march out, flashing their red cards at the judges.

And then I see the bald man with his Dalmatian.

"Hey, look!" Ned says, pointing. "I told you he'd be here."

I nod, because he did, and as the clock starts its countdown again, I realize Ned was right about how good the Dalmatian is at tricks and how much better all the dogs are than Kevin.

There's a Pomeranian that walks on its front paws, and a Staffordshire bull terrier that balances a ball on its nose as it rises up onto its back paws, and a border collie that jumps through super small hoops, and a small white dog that clambers up its owner's body to stand on their shoulders and then on their head.

Kevin can't do any of those things, and I start to think that entering the Happiest contest was the best idea because I would never have won the Obedience or Tricks trophies.

Derek goes back to pointing and saying "Wow," but I mostly keep my eyes on the Dalmatian, amazed by how many tricks he can do. I think he will win, even though all the dogs are fantastic.

When the buzzer sounds, the contest ends and everyone claps. Mindy checks the time on her phone and tells Derek and me that we have to get moving to meet our mums and then go to arena four to prepare for our contest. Kevin climbs to his feet and stretches, sticking his butt in the air and making a groaning sound. Ned presses a hand to my shoulder and asks me if I'm okay and ready, and I nod. Derek drags Vinnie out from under the seat again, prying another wrapper from his mouth, and leads the way along the row of seats and down the steps.

My heart is back to thumping hard and my ears are once again picking up all the sounds of people talking and laughing and dogs barking and growling and announcements and music and clapping and cheering, but I focus on Derek in front of me and the smell of Ned behind me and the feeling of Kevin's fur on my leg, and I feel ready.

Ready to win my trophy.

CHAPTER TWENTY-THREE

Derek and Vinnie are eight people in front of me as we stand and wait outside arena four with contestants twenty-three to twenty-nine between us. I see Vinnie jumping up and spinning and weaving around Derek's legs and then Derek untangling Vinnie's legs from his leash.

And then the lady in a yellow jacket at the front waves her arms and says, "Off you go, and good luck!"

I stare hard at Kevin, who trots along beside me, my blue trainers striding in time with his four scampering paws as we step onto the green grass of the arena. I squeeze Ned's pink ball in my free hand, trying to remember the instructions the lady in the yellow jacket told us at the start, but I can't remember any of them and now I'm scared I'll mess up and everyone will stare at me.

I'm still watching Kevin when I catch the movement of a hand waving on my right and a voice saying "Hold up your number" to me, and I glance up at the Happiest contest entrants ahead of me and see them raising their purple cards. I copy them, locking my eyes on the back of my purple card so I don't have to see any of the judges looking at me.

The lady and her corgi in front of me stop, and so do Kevin and I, and then the booming voice over the loudspeaker tells us to take our positions, and all the other entrants scatter to different parts of the square. I tug Kevin and copy them, leading him to an empty space. My head is still down because I think if I look up and see all the people watching or the judges' faces or any of the other dogs my beaker will overflow and I will start to cry. Not because I'm sad but because I don't know how to feel and I wish I had my emoji chart here.

And then I hear the buzzer and I know this means the clock on the big screen has started counting down.

It's time.

I crouch down and unclip the leash from Kevin's collar and kiss him on the head. "Okay, boy, it's time to be happy." His ears prick forward and he tilts his head, and then his tail wags slowly like he understands. Maybe he does.

"We've practiced tricks and obedience," I say, "and you always look happy, so let's just do those. Can you do that?"

Kevin barks once, and I ruffle the curls on his head and stand up straight. I peer around at the other entrants and see dogs leaping and running and rolling around, the owners tickling their tummies and rolling balls and playing tug-of-war with rope and bones.

The dogs look happy, but I know Kevin can be happier.

"Jump," I say to Kevin, and because my right thigh still hurts, I hop on one leg to show him what to do, flicking my hand into the air. Kevin jumps and barks, and then I make a circle with my hand and he spins around on his back paws. "Yes!" I say. I hop again and he copies me, letting out another bark. I then throw his ball in the air, just a small throw like we practiced this morning, and he leaps up and catches it and runs to me and drops it into my hand. "Yes!" I say again, smiling wide and patting his back.

We carry on, running through all the moves we've practiced, and Kevin is so good and happy and I think I'm having the best time I've ever had because the smile on my face is so big it's starting to hurt my cheeks.

And then I spot Vinnie.

He's running around the other entrants and their

dogs, yapping over and over, *yap yap yap*, trying to catch all the balls and steal all the toys and bouncing up to the other owners on his back paws. Derek is chasing after him, Vinnie's leash dangling from his shorts pocket and dragging on the ground behind him. He's calling for Vinnie to come back but Vinnie isn't listening because he's having way too much fun.

Vinnie then spots Kevin and dashes over to us, and I hear laughter coming from all directions, from the seating area where Mum and Wilma and Ned and Mindy are sitting and also from the judges and the adults in yellow jackets.

Kevin looks up at me and I shrug because I'm not sure if we can help, and then Vinnie is here, circling with Kevin. They start pawing at each other and growling as they play, and Derek jogs over. His face is red but his expression is happy, not sad or mad like I thought it would be.

"Hey," he says. "Vinnie is so naughty. I didn't think I'd be able to stop him from running away. Thank goodness you and Kevin are here."

"Aren't you angry with him?" I ask, because I don't think Vinnie is allowed to be naughty with all the judges watching.

Derek shakes his head. "Nah. Vinnie's having fun, which is cool."

I look back at our dogs, who are still playing, wrestling on the ground and then bounding up and circling again. The man's voice announces that there are ten seconds to go.

"Right, I'm going to catch him while he's in one place," Derek says. He hunches over, preparing the leash, and creeps toward our playing dogs, and then he rushes forward and hooks his hand into Vinnie's collar. Vinnie wiggles and wriggles and Derek stumbles and falls onto his knees, but he doesn't let go as he tries again and again to clip on Vinnie's leash.

I hear the crowd laughing louder as the buzzer sounds to announce the end of the contest, and I start to laugh too, slapping my thighs, because now Derek is lying on his back with Vinnie on his chest licking his cheek, and Kevin is licking the other cheek.

I wander over and call Kevin back, securing his leash to his collar, and then I reach out my hand, which Derek takes, and I pull him to his feet. He stands and looks around, his cheeks flushing even redder as he notices everyone laughing, and then they start clapping.

"How embarrassing," he says. Vinnie starts pulling him again and I follow them and all the other entrants toward the exit, holding up our purple cards once more.

Kevin nudges me with his wet nose, his tongue hanging out the side of his mouth, and I bend down and scratch behind his ears. "You were brilliant, Kevin," I say, and scoop him into my arms. I think I understand how Mum feels when she says she's proud of me, because that's how I feel about Kevin. As I exit the arena, I close my eyes and bury my face in Kevin's fur, listening to him puffing and panting.

I wait with Derek and Vinnie and Kevin in the starting area off to the side, and people keep coming up to Vinnie and patting his head and saying how funny he was. Derek smiles his one-sided smile at everyone, his cheeks still red, and Kevin stands in front of my feet, his side pressed tight against my shins. I stroke his back and then see Mum rushing over, putting her hair up in a ponytail at the same time. Wilma is right behind her with Ned and Mindy.

"Oh sweetie," Mum says, putting her arm around me and squatting down to kiss Kevin on the head. "You guys were so amazing!"

I nod and smile, my lips tight together. Kevin licks Mum's hand and wags his tail, and then Ned comes up and pats my shoulder before stroking Kevin on his sides with both hands. Kevin licks Ned's nose and Ned says, "Nice job, Kev, you did good."

Happiness is all I can feel inside me at the moment, and then my tummy rumbles and I realize I'm hungry because I didn't eat all of my porridge this morning.

Wilma wraps her arm around Mum's shoulder and smiles at me. "Your dog is brilliant," she says. "Not like our naughty monster." As she says it Vinnie drags Derek over to where we stand and everyone laughs.

"We need to get out of here," Mindy says, glancing over her shoulder. "I think the next contest is about to begin."

"Well, in that case," Wilma says, clapping her hands together, "why don't we all go get some lunch?"

"Great idea!" Derek says.

"What do you say? Hungry?" Mum asks.

I nod and ask, "Can we have hot dogs?" We head back out to the pathways that connect all the arenas and tents, where families and their dogs wander, enjoying the show.

"Who's that woman?" I hear Ned ask Mindy. I turn to see who he's talking about, but there are too many people everywhere, and I don't care anyway because I'm happy and now all I can think about is eating.

CHAPTER TWENTY-FOUR

My tummy is stuffed full of hot dogs and chips, and Kevin and Vinnie are lying side by side underneath the white table, licking their lips and paws and snuffling their noses in the grass looking for fallen food scraps.

Mum and Wilma are chatting about hair and holidays and Swedish food, and Ned and Mindy are talking quietly. I can't hear what they're saying, but they have their phones out and keep showing each other things on them and giggling and smiling. The sun is shining now, and I like the feel of the hot sun on my skin.

I take a sip from my water bottle and catch movement out of the corner of my eye as someone approaches. I take a peek and see that it's Angel and her older sister. She gives me a wave, her fingers wiggling in the air, and I sit up straighter in my chair that matches the table.

"Hey, Alex," she says.

"Hi, Angel," I reply. Her hair is super shiny in the sunlight.

Kevin clambers out from under the table and sniffs at Angel's leather sandals and feet. "Is this your dog?" she asks, crouching to stroke Kevin's head. Kevin sits and points his nose in the air, his ears flopping back, and Angel starts tickling his chest and tummy.

"Yep. This is Kevin. He likes that," I say.

"He is the cutest dog ever," she says. Her sister crouches down and starts petting Kevin too.

Vinnie scoots out from under the table in their direction, but he doesn't get far because Derek has his leash wrapped around the leg of his chair. Vinnie yaps and Angel looks at him and says, "Awwwww."

"Sorry," Derek says, scratching Vinnie's neck and pushing his bottom down, trying to make him sit.

"You're from school, aren't you?" Angel asks.

"Yeah, I'm Derek, Alex's friend. We live on the same road," he says. "Are you Alex's friend too?"

Angel nods. "Yes, we sit together in class and Alex shares his art things with me."

My eyes are wide, my hands flat and pressing into my thighs, and I glance from Angel to Derek.

Angel said I was her friend. And so did Derek.

My chest feels strange.

They said I'm their friend. They both said it. To each other. It must be real.

And now Angel is telling Derek about my amazing drawings and Derek is talking about how good I am at training Kevin and at *OrbsWorld*, and I don't know where to look or what to think. Kevin's front paws land on my knees, and he cranes his neck and points his head so he can reach my nose with his tongue, *lick lick lick*. I hold on to his neck with both hands and repeat Angel and Derek's words in my head, focusing on the feel of Kevin's wet tongue and his stinky hot breath.

They said I'm their friend.

"Okay, good luck in the contest," Angel says, tapping the back of my chair. I look up at her, into her dark eyes, and smile and nod.

"Thank you," I say, and Angel says, "See you Monday," and then she links arms with her sister and they walk off together, Angel's long glittery pink dress floating out behind her.

Derek goes back to eating his chips, dipping them in the red sauce, and I notice Ned returning to his table with two cans of lemonade, placing one in front of Mindy and sipping from the other. Mum and Wilma are still chatting, Mum throwing her head back and laughing, their hands touching now and then.

Friends.

Mum said good things come from bad things. At school last week and even this morning when we were late for registration, things were really bad. But now I think Mum's right, because Ned is happy and Mum is happy and Derek and Angel said I was their friend.

Those are all good things.

"Hi, Alex."

I only just hear the voice over the thoughts in my head and the sound of the music and the voices of other people all around me, because it's a quiet voice. I turn and see Jared and Isaac and Rahul approaching. Kevin hops off my knees and faces Jared, paws spread evenly like he's in the middle of running, his ears forward and his tail stiff and straight like a stick. Derek shifts in his chair, sliding his legs to the side to face Jared as well.

I haven't spoken to Jared since what he said at school and my insides feel twisted and swirly.

All three of them wear similar clothes: blue jeans, white T-shirts, and white caps with black logos on the front. I can't tell what the logo is. And then I notice another boy a little ways behind them wearing the same clothes, but his cap is black and is pulled lower over his face. Even though I can't see his face, I know it's Ryan.

"Hi, Alex," Jared says again, and Isaac and Rahul say hi too.

"Hi," I say, but my voice croaks so I glance down at Kevin and place my hand on his back.

"So, me and Ryan were talking, and we think that you should be in our group at districts."

I look up, my tummy squeezing and my breath hitching, and I frown at Jared, who's got his hands on his hips and is kicking the tip of his toe into the grass.

They want me to go to districts with them?

I glance at Derek, who's looking at me but not smiling, his blond hair dangling over his eyes, and then I look over at Ryan, who's also not smiling, but I can definitely see his dark eyes staring right at me.

My brain is full of thoughts and words so I breathe in deeply and think think think hard.

I could go to districts. And then out of nowhere I remember Ryan's face after he ran so fast and helped my group tie for first with Ella B.'s group. He was a good boy that day and he looked happy, and I've never seen Jared that happy before either. And maybe if I had raced that day, our last relay practice of the year, Jared wouldn't have crossed the line under the time limit and our team wouldn't have made districts.

Because I'm not as fast at running as the others.

I grind my back teeth together and rub a hand on my sore thigh. I do want to go to districts and I do want to be a fast runner, but maybe that's not how things are supposed to be.

"Nah, it's okay," I say, my eyes hopping from Jared to Ryan. "Ryan should run because he's much faster than me."

Jared clears his throat and his hands fidget as he turns to frown at Isaac and Rahul. "Erm, really? Are you sure?" he asks.

I nod because I am sure. "Yeah, Ryan should go with you."

Jared smiles and shoves his hands in his pockets. "Okay, well, thanks. And your dog's really cute, by the way. You should have told a story about him at school yesterday. I bet you have some good ones."

I nod again and don't know what to say, and I think that maybe next time Ms. Westing asks, I might put up my hand and share a story. Maybe.

"Okay, so, bye," Jared says, and he strides away

with Isaac and Rahul following. I spy Ryan's red trainers with white laces and black stripes shuffling nearer. Kevin moves sideways to stand between us.

I don't have my cap on, so I know that Ryan can't whack it off, but I wonder what he might do instead. I hope Kevin doesn't bite him because Kevin's never bitten anyone, but I can hear him grumbling, really low and quiet.

Ryan stops and stays quiet for a moment until I look up at him, and then he says, "Thanks for letting me run," and then he grins and waves and runs off to catch up with Jared.

"Well, that was weird," Derek says.

I turn to face Derek as he starts munching on another chip, and I think that his food must be cold by now.

He's right, that was weird, but I don't have time to think about it anymore because the music suddenly shuts off and a woman's voice starts blaring out of all the speakers at once.

"This is your five-minute warning," she says. "Yes, that's five minutes until the presentation of trophies begins in the main display area."

The music comes back on, pounding drumbeats and strumming guitars and a girl's voice singing, and chatter and barking floods my ears. My hands shake and my chest tightens as Mum and Wilma, Ned and Mindy, and Derek all stand at the same time and start clearing the tables of all our rubbish. They're all talking to me but I can't hear their words.

Kevin hops on my lap and rests his head on my shoulder, and I hug him.

"It's trophy time," I whisper in his ear, and he huffs and licks his lips and then my face. I hug him tighter and stand, putting Kevin on the ground, and I walk with my family and Derek's family toward the display area.

CHAPTER TWENTY-FIVE

The main display area is another square of grass surrounded by a fence that's really just thick red tape attached to short poles stuck in the ground, but it's larger than the others and is situated right beside Jessops Lake. The sky is so big and blue without a single cloud anywhere, and the sun continues to beat down, making the top of the water look like it's made of diamonds. I can smell coconut as Mum rubs something wet—sunscreen—into the back of my neck.

In the middle of the display area is a small stage. The hugest TV screen I've ever seen hangs above the stage, and I know that's so everyone in the crowd can see the people on the stage clearly. Right now it shows tables set up with heaps of gold and silver trophies in rows and adults in smart suits and others in yellow jackets walking back and forth. A song blasts from the speakers about being simply the best, and I think that's a really good song to play now because we're all about to see which dogs were the best.

I hold on to Kevin a bit tighter, his front legs dangling over my arm, pulling him even closer to my body. We're surrounded by people and dogs on all sides and I'm in the middle of our group—Mum and Wilma behind, Ned and Mindy in front, and Derek and Vinnie to my right.

Vinnie is trying to play with a black Labrador who's sitting in front of us, facing the stage. He's batting a paw against the dog's butt, but the dog isn't turning around to face him, and I think it's because the Lab is old and probably doesn't like playing games like that anymore. Derek keeps pulling Vinnie back and telling him no, but Vinnie isn't listening, and I think Kevin is enjoying watching them.

The song fades away and is replaced by the woman's voice from before, and I clench my back teeth together because this is it.

"Welcome, everyone, to the final presentations of this year's PAWS Dog Show!"

The crowd erupts into clapping and cheering and I can't breathe, even though I'm excited, because the noise is too loud. I squeak and then Ned takes Kevin from my arms so I can put my hands over my ears. The noise still gets through my hands but it's dull now and doesn't hurt or make my brain feel confused.

Mum taps my shoulder, and I remove my hands and listen again to the woman's voice, and then I tilt my head around the Labrador's family so I can see the TV screen. The woman is on the screen, microphone in hand, and she's wandering up and down in front of the table of trophies and introducing herself as Betty Frisp, and I wonder if she might be my art teacher's sister. She says how thankful she is for such an amazing turnout and what a fabulous day it's been and how much she loves all the different dogs and how brilliant it is that the sun came out.

Everyone laughs and claps, and I hover my hands over my ears in case it all gets too loud again. Mum asks if I want to leave but I shake my head because I want to see which dogs have won the trophies.

"Right, let's start announcing the winners!" Betty Frisp says, and I watch her on the screen as she turns and picks up a small piece of paper in front of the farthest trophy on the right. "And the winner of the Agility contest goes to . . . Fred the collie and his owner Fiona, pink entrant number fourteen!"

The crowd cheers and whoops and dogs bark and whine and I ram my hands back over my ears, but I keep my eyes open so I can see Fred and Fiona walk up onto the stage.

Fiona is young, maybe still a teenager but an older one, and Fred bounds along beside her on his leash as they climb the stairs to the stage and collect their silver trophy. The audience cheers again as Fiona and Fred stand beside Betty Frisp and people start snapping photos. And then Fiona shakes Betty Frisp's hand and takes a white envelope from her before turning and leaving the stage.

The noise from the crowd dies down and Betty Frisp talks again.

"Fantastic," she says. "Right, on we go with the winner of the Shiniest Coat contest . . ."

For the next ten minutes she calls out the winners' names, and they all go up to the stage to collect their trophies and envelopes as the crowd shouts and claps. I smile and stamp my feet when the bald man and his Dalmatian are announced as winners of the Tricks contest because I know he deserves to win that trophy.

Vinnie has stopped attacking the Lab's butt and is now lying on his back at Derek's feet with his paws in the air, wriggling from side to side and trying to catch his tail. Kevin lies still in Ned's arms with one paw on my arm, staring at me. Ned doesn't complain once about holding him, and even though I know everyone keeps talking to me, I don't answer or even hear what they say because the more Betty Frisp talks, the more scared and nervous I feel inside.

"Okay, moving on," Betty Frisp says after taking a drink from a bottle of water. She picks up a piece of paper in front of another silver trophy. "And the winner of the Happiest contest is . . ."

I don't think I'm breathing, and my tummy has turned into a rock, and my body feels heavy, and I can't blink.

And then Wilma and Mum and Mindy and Ned are cheering and jumping and clapping, and Derek's mouth has opened wide like he's screaming but no noise is coming out and his blue eyes are wide as well, his eyebrows high on his wrinkled forehead. He bends down and scoops up Vinnie from the ground, and he and Wilma start pushing through all the people and dogs in front of us who cheer and tickle Vinnie's tummy and pat Derek on the back as he passes.

I look down at my feet, hands on my ears, still not able to blink or breathe.

Kevin tries to climb over my arm to get to me,

but I can't move my hands. And then he's licking me and I shut my eyes and inhale in a gasp.

Mum is talking but I can't hear her because my brain is replaying the names Betty Frisp called out.

It wasn't my name.

It wasn't Kevin's name.

It was Vinnie and Derek.

CHAPTER TWENTY-SIX

I sit on the grass with Kevin curled up in my lap, his nose resting on my thigh and his eyes looking up at me. Mum and Ned and Mindy are sitting around me. I stare at my bare feet and at my trainers, which sit side by side beside me with my socks balled up inside.

I can't remember how we got here to the back of the audience, where there's more space, or when I took off my shoes, but I feel calmer now because most of the noise is away from me.

Kevin and I lock eyes and I breathe in and out, in and out, and I don't feel quite so dizzy anymore. Mum isn't touching me because when she tried I shook her off, but she's right next to me, and I can see her brown legs crossed at the ankles. Mindy and Ned are talking and Mindy keeps smiling at me, her pink lips glistening in the sun.

"Sorry," I say, because it's all my brain can think.

"What for?" Mum asks, and Ned and Mindy look at me.

"Sorry," I repeat and then inhale again, nice and deep, so my chest expands all big until it sticks out, and I glance up at Mindy. "Sorry for making you miss Derek getting his trophy."

Mindy smiles again, showing me her perfect white teeth, which are even whiter than her hair. "I'll be able to see it when I get home," she says, "because Derek set the box to record the whole show on TV." She laughs and smooths her long hair between her palms and over her shoulder. "I'm sure we will all have no choice but to watch it later."

I nod and feel better and hope that I can see Derek get his trophy as well. I also wonder if Vinnie is being a good boy up on the stage.

"I think Vinnie was the happiest dog," I say, looking back down at Kevin, who lifts his chin off my leg. "He was so happy he couldn't even be a good boy in the contest, not like you."

Ned snort-laughs and kicks my foot gently with his. "Vinnie was so funny, right?" I nod and we all laugh because now I remember Vinnie in arena four during the contest, and it is super funny in my head the way he charged around with his ears back, *yap yap yap*ping at everyone.

And then I see Vinnie galloping toward us, Derek tripping and stumbling along behind him and gripping tight to Vinnie's leash. Kevin stands and gives my face a couple of quick licks. Then he hops off my lap and goes to meet Vinnie, and they start their circling and growling game.

Wilma walks a little ways behind Derek, who plonks down beside me, and I notice her tall, thin frame slipping easily through the gaps between people. She's holding Derek's trophy. My tummy does a twist and I pull my knees up to my chest, planting my feet side by side, but then Derek is talking to me and I can't feel the twisting anymore.

"Are you okay?" he asks, and I look up into his blue eyes and nod. "Sorry I won and not you," he says, "because if I was judging, I'd have chosen Kevin as the winner." He pats Kevin's butt as he continues playing with Vinnie.

"Nah, I think Vinnie was definitely the happiest dog there today," I say. "I would have picked him."

Derek grins and then holds up a white envelope.

"What did you win?" Mindy asks.

Everyone leans forward as Derek opens it—even Vinnie and Kevin come over and sit—and we all watch his fingers as they slide out a small card. My eyes scan the words on the card at the same time as Derek reads them aloud.

"'Congratulations on being a PAWS winner.

This voucher entitles you to spend five hundred dollars at any Pet Pamperland store.'" Derek looks up at us all. "Wow, five hundred dollars?"

"Wow!" Wilma says, taking a seat beside Mum. "How will you ever spend all of this money in one shop? Perhaps you need someone to help you—and no, I do not mean you, Miss Shopaholic Mindy."

Mindy giggles and swats Wilma's foot, and I nod and clench my back teeth together because that is a lot of money and I think Derek could buy so many cool things for Vinnie in that store.

Vinnie sniffs the voucher and then sneezes three times in a row, *choo choo choo*, and Derek scratches Vinnie's ear and laughs. "Yeah, I agree, Vin," he says. I have no idea why he says this because Vinnie only sneezed and no dogs say human words.

Derek turns to face me again and smiles with the side of his mouth. "Want to share the voucher?" he asks.

I pause, replaying his question in my head, and then I make fists and look at Mum because I don't know if I'm allowed.

She makes a strange face where her eyebrows rise and her lips draw in together, and I wish I knew what it meant. But then she nods and says, "Derek, are you sure?"

"Yeah, definitely. I think Vinnie would want to share it with Kevin anyway," he answers, so I nod and say, "Thank you," and Derek pats me on the back. "Cool. Hey, Mum, can we go there tomorrow?"

Wilma shrugs and says, "I don't think that will be a problem. Would you like that, Alex, if you and Derek and your mum and I all go to this Pamperland place tomorrow to spend the voucher? And hey, how about afterward we head to our house for a Sunday dinner? I will cook!" She claps her hands once.

"And we can play *Skyscraper Escapades*!" Derek adds. "You have to bring your laptop."

"Yeah," I say as I suck in lots of air because I would like that so much.

"Do you want to see how much energy you have tomorrow before agreeing?" Mum asks.

I tilt my head, thinking. Being autistic and shy means sometimes I can get very tired when I'm around people and lots of noise and activity in busy places. But I think this time I'll definitely be okay to spend the day with Derek. So I nod and say, "No, I'll have enough energy."

I turn to Derek. "Thank you," I say, and scratch

behind Kevin's ears as he comes to sit between Derek and me.

"That's okay. It'll be cool."

I think Derek is cool.

And I remember what Mum said on Wednesday about her friends sharing things with her and making her feel better when she was sad, and I know it doesn't matter that I didn't win the trophy today because it turned out I didn't need it to make a friend.

I already have one.

Or two, because Angel called me her friend and she makes me feel better every day at school.

"Okay, so shall we head off?" Wilma says, and we all agree and stand up. Derek lets me hold his trophy, which is quite heavy and the shiniest silver I have ever seen. It has the picture of the Chinese crested dog on it and HAPPIEST etched into the curved part in the middle. It's amazing, and I know it will look even more amazing on Derek's shelf, and maybe it will make him smile when he looks at it instead of sad like when he looks at his fishing trophies.

We're moving toward the exit when Ned says, "Wait up," and we pause and look back toward the stage. Betty Frisp is talking again and introducing someone else. I can still see the TV screen and beside her stands the woman who was looking at me earlier, the one with the dark hair like mine and the skin that's darker and the clipboard.

"We decided to start a new contest this year, a very special secret one, and Krystal here"—Betty gestures toward the clipboard lady—"has been wandering around watching you all with your dogs. You might have seen her."

I nod because I did—I saw her a few times.

"Well, I shall hand things over to Krystal so she can tell you more."

Krystal takes the microphone from Betty and tucks her clipboard under her arm. The crowd is quiet, just a faint shushing and the occasional cough and bark, and everyone is facing the stage waiting to hear what Krystal has to say.

"Hi, everyone," Krystal says, her voice gentle and soft and clean. "So as Betty said, I had the pleasure of observing you all today with your beautiful dogs because I had the important job of picking one very special winner." Betty comes up beside Krystal, holding the handles of a big gold trophy, and Krystal smiles at her. "It wasn't easy, I promise, but there was one dog I saw today who stood out, and it was obvious to me that he should be the winner."

Mum and Wilma, Ned and Mindy, and Derek and I all glance at each other, and I can tell by everyone's faces that they're as excited as me because there has never been a secret contest at PAWS before. I pick Kevin up so he can see the stage and the screen, and so I don't slap my thighs because there are so many people around who might see. But he doesn't want to see the screen. He just rests his chin on my shoulder, his soft fur crushed against my neck and cheek.

"I asked around," Krystal continues, "and found out the name of this dog and his owner. I would like you all to give a big round of applause to the very first winner of the Best Dog Friend contest at PAWS."

"Best Dog Friend?" Derek repeats.

"Congratulations to Alex Freeman and his gorgeous cockapoo, Kevin!"

CHAPTER TWENTY-SEVEN

The crowd is clapping and cheering but all I can hear is Derek and Ned screaming and yelling and whooping and I don't mind that it's loud because my thoughts are too jumbled for me to focus on all the noise.

That was my name. Mine and Kevin's.

"Please come up to the stage and collect your trophy and your prize when you're ready, Alex," I hear Krystal say. And then Mum, who's crying, and Ned are wrapping their arms around me and Kevin, who's still in my arms, and are gently pushing me forward through the people and toward the stage, saying things in my ears. My eyes are fixed on Kevin's fur because I know if I peek up even a tiny bit I will see faces looking at me and I still don't know what's happening inside my head and my body.

We reach the red tape that wraps around the display area and there's a walkway through the middle that goes right up to the stage steps with more red tape on either side. Kevin, Mum, Ned, and I are walking up this pathway now, toward the stage, and I remember that I don't have my shoes on, and the grass is soft and scratchy at the same time and I wonder if people are looking at my bare feet. Mum is gripping my shoulder and Ned is saying "How cool is this" over and over, and I focus on them and on Kevin in my arms and the way he's so still and pressed against my skin.

And then we're at the stage and I'm walking up the steps, my feet thudding against the warm wooden blocks until I'm at the top, and then I see Krystal and Betty Frisp right in front of me and I stand still, squeezing Kevin tighter.

"You must be Alex," Betty says, and she crouches down so she can see into my eyes because I'm looking down at everyone's legs and feet and the dark wood of the stage.

Krystal appears next and I look up at her face and notice the wrinkles at the sides of her eyes and how her skin looks like someone has put glitter all over it. "Alex, it's such a pleasure to meet you," she says, and I nod. Her eyes then shift down to Kevin and she asks if she can pet him and I nod again. Her long fingers gently stroke from his head to his tail, and he lifts his head from my shoulder and licks her hand. "Oh, thank you," she says to him, and he licks her some more.

Betty stands behind Krystal, the huge gold trophy in her arms, and I notice how I can see reflections in the gold and the words BEST DOG FRIEND, PAWS engraved on the front.

A trophy that Kevin and I have won.

I don't know if I have space on my desk for it.

"Alex, as soon as I first saw you, I knew you and Kevin had something special," Krystal tells me. I nod and peek up at her wrinkly eyes again. She's not smiling as big now but the wrinkles are still there. "I think Kevin is the best friend anyone could ever ask for, and I think you are very lucky to have each other."

I nod and say thank you but the words don't really come out because my mouth feels numb and all I can think about is Kevin in my arms and what Angel and Ms. Westing will say to me when they find out. Kevin looks at me and I stare back and think about how if Kevin hadn't run away that day to meet Vinnie, I might not have made friends with Derek, or Mum with Wilma, and maybe Ned would never have spoken to Mindy. I think I might be crying but I can't be sure and I don't care because today is the best day ever.

"Shall I give the trophy to Mum?" Betty Frisp asks, and I nod because my hands are busy holding Kevin. I watch Mum take it with both her hands and say it's heavier than she expected.

And then Betty crouches again and this time I look at her old face. She looks just like Ms. Frisp but maybe her face is a bit rounder and her hair a bit lighter.

"You know what, Alex?" she says, placing her hands on her bent knees. "I have a confession to make." I don't know what a confession is but it sounds like Betty has something serious to tell me. "I actually heard your name before today."

I frown at this, wondering how she could know my name.

"And here's a secret that not many people know . . ." Betty leans in closer. "You know how we have an art contest every year to choose the PAWS logo for the following year?" I nod again. "The judge of that competition is my sister, who is your art teacher at school—you know Ms. Frisp?" I nod because I do and I was right; I knew that Betty looked like Ms. Frisp and they are sisters. "Uh-huh, well, Ms. Frisp isn't here today because she doesn't like dogs all that much."

"She likes cats," I say.

"Doesn't she just. Well, anyway, Ms. Frisp chose one of your sketches as the winning entry this year."

I frown, wondering what she's talking about because I didn't enter the competition and I don't share my artwork at school with anyone but Angel. And then I remember my green robot notebook and how Ms. Frisp wanted to keep it until Friday.

"But Ms. Frisp has asked me to ask you first, because you didn't enter the contest officially and she knows you like to keep your art a secret. So, would that be okay?" I look into Betty's gray eyes and then at Mum beside me and I don't know what to say, but then I do. I have a question.

"Which sketch?"

Betty stands up and plods in her big clumpy trainers over to the table, then picks up a piece of paper from the back. "Ms. Frisp made a copy from your notebook," she says as she comes back.

I look at the paper. It's the last one I did in the robot notebook, the one I think is the best sketch I've ever drawn in my life.

It's Kevin with his paw on top of a trophy.

She holds it up, and Kevin turns his head and looks at it too, sniffing the white page, and then he licks it.

Betty laughs. "I think that's a yes from Kevin," she says. "But what do you say, Alex?"

I think hard about all the people who will see the sketch, how it will be all over the posters and the trophies and even on TV. Everyone will see Kevin and the trophy and I realize that this is a good thing, and it makes me feel happy and excited and proud.

This is the best day of my life.

So I nod and give Kevin the biggest hug I've ever given him.

ACKNOWLEDGMENTS

It's hard to describe how surreal it is to be writing an acknowledgments page, yet here I am. Reaching this point in my career has been quite a journey, and I have so many people to thank for keeping me on my path—I've stumbled and fallen off countless times!

To my publishers and editors, Linsay Knight, Clare Hallifax, Kristina Schulz, Frances Taffinder, Carter Hasegawa, and their amazing teams. Knowing how much *All the Small Wonderful Things* means to you all is a feeling like no other. I received such a warm welcome into Team Walker and Team Candlewick, and to have a dedicated and wonderful group of professionals work together to bring Alex and Kevin's story to life is a feeling unmatched.

An enormous heartfelt thank-you to Chloe Davis and the Darley Anderson Children's Book Agency team. I would be lost without you. To Alice Sutherland-Hawes, Judy Roberts, Lynn Leitch, Jessica Vitalis, Katrin Dreiling, J. C. Davis,

Tammy Oja, Bella Ellwood-Clayton, Ellie Terry, and Wendy Orr for your time, kind words, and invaluable encouragement. To Matthew at Salt and Sage Books, my sensitivity readers, and the editors at the Ink and Insights contest. To my mum and husband for reading and understanding the importance of this story and what it means to me and our family. Thank you all so much.

Thank you to every single one of my writer buddies who read chapters of this book and supported me through the ups and downs of querying and submission, and to the 21ders debut group for sharing your passion, love, and experiences so openly. Only writers truly understand what this business is like on the inside!

Finally, to you, the amazing reader for whom this book was written. I hope *All the Small Wonderful Things* brings you as much love and joy as it's brought me. And be sure to pat all the dogs and thank them for their service. They make the world a better place.

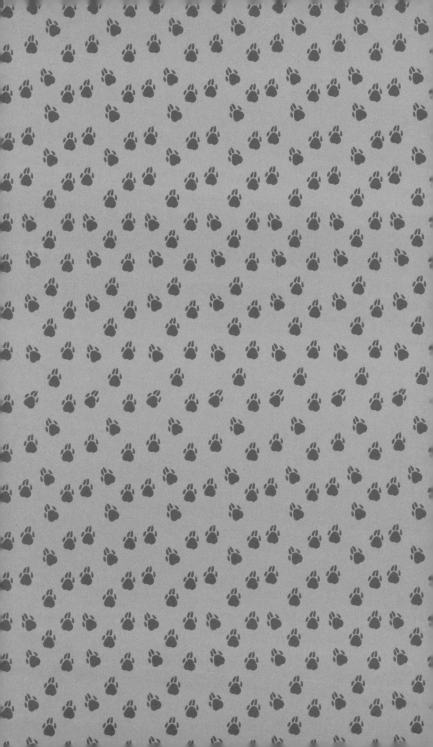